PLENTY TO B

Plenty, FL 5

Lara Valentine

MENAGE EVERLASTING

Siren Publishing, Inc.
www.SirenPublishing.com

A SIREN PUBLISHING BOOK
IMPRINT: Ménage Everlasting

PLENTY TO BELIEVE
Copyright © 2013 by Lara Valentine

ISBN: 978-1-62740-612-3

First Printing: December 2013

Cover design by Les Byerley
All art and logo copyright © 2013 by Siren Publishing, Inc.

Printed in the U.S.A.

PUBLISHER
Siren Publishing, Inc.
www.SirenPublishing.com

PLENTY TO BELIEVE

Plenty, FL 5

LARA VALENTINE
Copyright © 2013

Chapter One

Leah was a mess. A complete and total mess. It was Monday morning, almost ten o'clock, and her heart was beating fast and her palms were sweaty. She smoothed her hands down her navy-blue slacks and pushed her glasses up her nose for the thousandth time already today.

Justin Reynolds and Linc Davis were due to visit her bookstore any minute. They came every Monday morning at ten to browse for books, chat with her, and lately, bring her a large sweet tea from the diner. She was the very picture of pathetic with her crush on these handsome, sexy men. They could have their pick of women within a two-hundred-mile radius, and often did. Women were always showing up at their nightclub, Party Like A Rock Star, and throwing themselves at the two men. At their Halloween party last fall, Linc had a blonde hanging off each arm. Seeing him with them had cut her heart to the quick. She had left shortly after, not wanting to see any more.

She knew they'd never look at a woman like her, but she didn't need constant reminders of the fact. The women they dated had voluptuous figures and had perfected a certain bored, yet simpering expression on their perfectly made-up faces.

Leah, on the other hand, had a slim, almost boyish figure. No special push-up bra was going to make anyone describe her as curvy or lush. Her face was ordinary and she rarely wore more makeup other than mascara and a little lip gloss. She could never look as bored either. She found life fascinating, and had an unquenchable thirst to learn about anything and everything.

The bell above the door rang and it jangled her already stretched nerves. She couldn't stop her smile as the two sexiest men in Plenty entered. She could feel her body respond instantly, humming to life like a diesel engine.

"Morning, Leah. How was your weekend? Did you do anything interesting?"

Justin was smiling, his golden-boy good looks dazzling. He was wearing faded blue jeans and a black T-shirt. Linc followed behind, Justin's total opposite with dark hair and eyes, also dressed in jeans, but with a button-down shirt. He was not quite making eye contact with her. He was much more quiet and reserved, but not unfriendly. Just introverted, like herself. She much preferred an evening in with a good book or movie to a loud party with a bunch of people.

Justin handed her the tall iced tea and their fingers brushed, sending tingles of electricity straight up her arm.

"Thanks, you guys spoil me. I love the sweet tea from the diner. And no, I didn't do anything exciting. I spent Saturday at the library. I volunteer for their literacy program. I tutor kids who are having trouble learning to read."

"I didn't ask if you did anything exciting. I asked if you did anything interesting. That sounds pretty interesting to me. I'd heard you did volunteer work but I didn't realize what it was. That must be very rewarding."

"Maybe I'm selfishly creating a new generation of customers for my store."

Justin shook his head. "You couldn't be selfish if you tried. Your heart is too soft. Right, Linc?"

Linc finally smiled, but it didn't look as genuine as Justin's. "True. You're the last old-fashioned girl, Leah. I bet you baked them cupcakes, too."

Leah's spine stiffened. Linc was making fun of her. "Cookies. Now let me show you the new books this week. I think there's a couple you might be interested in."

She walked briskly to the front of the store, not glancing back to see if they were following her. Linc grabbed her arm, turning her around so she was facing him. He looked like Lucifer, dangerous as sin with his dark hair, dark eyes, and goatee. This time his eyes were soft and warm. She hated herself for the shiver running up her arm at his touch.

"Leah, if what I said offended you, I'm sorry. I didn't mean it that way. I meant it as a compliment."

She was never one to hold a grudge. Her anger was gone as quickly as it had come. She forced a smile, fighting the urge to trace his lips with her fingers.

"I'm sorry, too. I guess I got up on the wrong side of the bed this morning. I stayed up too late watching an old movie."

"What movie?" Justin picked up a hardback from the display.

"*The Thin Man*. William Powell and Myrna Loy."

Linc's face split into a grin and it took her breath away. He wasn't as happy go lucky as Justin and he smiled less often. "One of my favorites. I've seen all *The Thin Man* movies. Do you like *Citizen Kane*?"

"I love it. One of my favorites. You like old movies, too? I have a book somewhere over here about the Golden Age of Hollywood." Leah bustled over to a shelf and leafed through the books. Justin was whispering something to Linc, and Linc was shaking his head. Linc looked frustrated, but Justin looked unperturbed. She found the book and showed it to Linc. "It focuses mostly on when talkies started all the way to the demise of the studio system."

Linc perused the back cover and nodded. "I'll take this one."

"So, Leah," Justin began. "What are you doing for dinner tomorrow night?"

Linc immediately walked to the back of the store and began browsing through the historical biography section. She dragged her attention back to Justin.

"Um, I don't know. Probably a frozen dinner in front of the television. Why?"

Justin pulled a face. "That sounds terrible. I—I mean, we were wondering if you might want to come over for dinner tomorrow night. Tuesday's the day you close early, right?"

It was. She usually spent the afternoon biking around the quarries if the weather was good, and inside reading a good book if the weather was bad. Sometimes, she would hang out with her cousin Jason, if he was off duty. He worked as a deputy in Plenty.

"Yes, I close at one o'clock on Tuesdays."

The bell over the door and she turned to see one of her best customers, Jillian Parks, enter the store. She waved to Jillian. "Be with you in a minute." Jillian nodded and started to look through the best-seller endcap.

Leah turned back to Justin, who was waiting patiently for an answer. She wasn't sure what to say to his dinner invitation. He had never invited her to his home before. Everyone knew he and Linc had a huge house on the outskirts of town near their nightclub, but few had been invited there.

Her silence must have indicated she wasn't sure. "Do you already have plans? I can assure you I'm a good cook. I took cooking lessons from a famous Italian chef whom I can't name because of some confidentiality agreement, but he taught me a great deal."

"You want me to come for dinner? Why?"

She hadn't meant to blurt it out like that, but she couldn't help but wonder what prompted this uncharacteristic display.

Justin reached out and tucked a strand of her reddish-brown hair behind her ear, sending a streak of heat straight to her pussy.

"Because we like you. We've gotten to know each other pretty well, wouldn't you say? We get along and enjoy talking. How about talking over a meal? I promise I won't make you marry me at the end of the evening."

His smile was teasing, but he had no idea just how many women in the world had probably fantasized that very thing. She hadn't, of course. She was too practical for something like that, but she knew many had.

Justin was so handsome and sexy, and she was so smitten, there was no way she was going to say no. She couldn't have turned him down if her life depended on it.

"If you're sure I won't have to marry you, then I'll come. I love Italian food. What time should I be there? Is there anything I can bring?"

"How about sevenish? If you want to bring something, you can bring dessert. My skills don't stretch to baking or sweets."

She glanced over her shoulder and saw Jillian pretending to page through a Stephen King, but knew she was taking the scene in with interest.

"Okay, I'll bring dessert. If you'll excuse me?" She nodded to Jillian, and Justin smiled and headed to the back of the store with Linc. She marched over to Jillian and plucked the book from her hand.

"You've read it. Stop pretending you weren't listening."

Jillian grinned. "I love small towns. Gossip wasn't nearly this good in Chicago." Jillian waggled her eyebrows. "You dark horse. I had no idea you, Justin, and Linc were so *friendly*. Good for you. They need a nice girl, not like some of those ho-bags that hang out at the club in skimpy outfits hoping to sleep with a rock star."

"Former rock star." Truth was, Leah didn't really think of Justin as a rock star. He acted like an ordinary, nice guy.

Jillian shrugged. "Former, then. Is this the first date for you three? A candlelit dinner. So romantic."

Leah held up her hand. Things seemed to be spiraling out of her control. "First of all, he never said it was a romantic, candlelit dinner. He said it was dinner. It may not even be a date. Period. Second, well, I don't know what the second thing is but I'll think of it. It's just dinner."

Jillian looked excited. "We should go shopping. Maybe get your hair done." She started to pull her cell phone from her purse, but Leah stopped her.

"No. I'm just going as me."

Jillian pouted but put her phone back in her purse. "Okay. If you say so."

"I say so. Now why are you here on a Monday morning?"

"School's closed for Presidents' Day. Did you forget to send your Presidents' Day cards to friends and family?"

Leah laughed. "I'm afraid I did. How remiss of me. What can I help you with then?"

"I need a cookbook for Ava. God love her, she's trying to learn to cook for her men. I think it may be a lost cause, though."

Ava and her three men, Brayden, Josh, and Falk, had just gotten engaged on Valentine's Day and were already planning an autumn wedding.

"Follow me. I think I have something which might help a beginner."

Leah led the way down the aisle, close to where Justin and Linc were deep in conversation. She was about to pull the cookbook down from the shelf when she overheard Justin's and Linc's voices. Justin's voice was soft and even, while Linc's was hushed and angry. She caught Linc's clipped tones and almost crawled under the shelves.

"I don't want to have dinner with Leah, dammit. I'm not interested in her. She's not my type."

She felt her breath catch. Linc didn't like her so much he didn't even want to share a simple meal with her. Tears pricked the back of her eyes and a lump formed in her throat. She straightened her shoulders. She already knew she wasn't Lincoln Davis's type. She'd seen the scantily clad centerfold types hanging off his arm. She turned back to Jillian with her head held high.

"I think Ava will really like this one. It's for a beginner and it has lots of pictures of the recipes as it's made, not just the final product."

Jillian was biting her lip, and Leah hated the expression of pity on her face. "Thanks, I'll get this one. Listen, why don't you join us for dinner at the diner tonight? Cassie, Becca, Ava, and myself all get together every Monday night."

Leah shook her head. She wanted to crawl away somewhere and lick her wounds. Besides, she never knew what to say when a conversation wasn't one-on-one. Too many people made her nervous and tongue tied.

Maybe she should call her cousin Jason and spend the evening with him. She needed to talk to him, preferably soon. Telling him the news that her brother, Gabe, was finally coming back home was going to be traumatic for him. They'd been so close until a few years ago. She still didn't know everything that had happened to rip their friendship apart, but she knew it had been painful on both sides.

Jillian linked their arms as they headed toward the cash register. "I'm not taking no for an answer. Be there tonight or I'll come to your place and drag you out by your drool-worthy hair. I mean it."

Leah's hand flew to the top of her head. "It's not drool worthy."

"Yes, it is. It's thick, shiny, and has the most amazing mix of brown, gold, and red. I don't even know what color to call it, but it's gorgeous."

"It's reddish brown, I guess. And it's too thick. If I put it up on the top of my head, I get headaches."

"To have such problems. We'll see you tonight. Don't make me come after you." Jillian put her hand on Leah's arm. "You'll have fun. Don't sit at home and think about that no-good rat, Linc Davis."

Linc wasn't a rat, just honest.

She rang up Jillian's book and Justin and Linc came to the counter to pay for their books.

Linc handed her his credit card, and gave Justin an evil grin. "Happy birthday. The books are on me."

Leah smiled when Justin cringed. "It's your birthday? Happy birthday, Justin."

"Actually, my birthday was Saturday and Linc got me a gift already, but I'm happy to let him buy these books, too. In fact, you can buy me another coffee. I need the caffeine."

Jillian headed out the door as Justin handed over several books they'd found. She tried not to look at Linc as she ran his credit card, handing him his slip.

Justin tucked the bag under his arm. "I'll see you tomorrow night."

Her gaze flew to Linc. He wasn't looking at her, studying a rack of childbirth books he couldn't have any real interest in. She took a deep breath. He wasn't going to keep her from having dinner with Justin. He seemed genuine in his friendship and his desire to want her there.

"Tomorrow night. Sevenish." She smiled at Justin, ignoring Linc.

After they exited the store, Leah slumped against the counter. If Justin and Linc truly wanted to share a woman, going to dinner was a really stupid thing to do. She would end up heartbroken when Justin moved on to a woman they both agreed on.

But she couldn't stop herself from spending time with them. Both of them. She was drawn to them like the proverbial bee to honey, magnet to steel. She tried to be philosophical. She'd never had her heart broken. It was probably way past time.

* * * *

Justin handed Linc his coffee. They were sitting in Josh's Java after their shopping trip to Leah's bookstore. Linc wasn't in the fucking mood to talk and it was clear Justin was frustrated as hell with his best friend.

"Why are you acting this way? I know you're attracted to her. Not your type my ass. I see the way you look at her when she's not watching."

Linc scowled over his coffee. "You're seeing things, buddy. Leah's not my type. You know I like them blonde, busty, and uncomplicated. Leah's complicated. She's got 'complicated' written all over her."

"If that's your way of saying she's smarter than hell, you're right. I like a woman who knows how to spell her own name and doesn't dot the 'i' with a little heart or flower."

Linc smirked. "Are you saying the ladies I date are dumb? I'm not attracted to their scintillating conversation. I have you for that."

"I don't think you're attracted to them at all. I think Leah is your type. She's my type and we're attracted to the same women."

Linc stretched out his long legs. "She doesn't look like the women we've dated in the past."

That, at least, was the truth. Leah was infinitely more beautiful than any woman he'd had in his life before. She was petite, her body slight. Linc guessed she barely weighed a hundred pounds soaking wet. Her hips were rounded, but trim, her bottom a sweet, sexy curve. Her breasts were small and firm, but the perfect size for his hand. Her skin was creamy, damn near perfect. Her eyes were a soft, warm brown that made a man's heart pound and his stomach twist into knots. Her lips were full and he'd fought the urge to kiss her dozens of times. He could get lost gazing at her beautiful face, his hand stroking her shiny, gorgeous hair. It was the most unusual color and looked like silk. He wanted to rub the strands between his fingers and bury his face in her neck, breathing in her sweet scent.

He wasn't going to do any of those things.

Justin sipped his coffee. "Exactly. I'm done with casual sex and women who are only in it to be with someone famous. I want a real relationship, with a real woman. I want someone I can love and build a family with. I thought that's what you wanted, too. It's what we talked about when we moved here."

It was what they talked about. Linc wanted the love of a good woman as much, maybe even more, than Justin did. The woman simply couldn't be Leah, although he couldn't imagine himself with anyone else. His attraction to her was strong. He liked and respected her, too. She was the kind of woman a man was proud of, and would want her to be proud of him in return.

"When we find the right woman, I want those things. All of them. The right woman isn't Leah. I'm sorry." Linc stared out the front window of the coffee shop, watching the residents of Plenty pass by. He loved this damn town. He'd chosen well when he'd told Justin they should move here.

"Listen, you really seem to have feelings for Leah. If you want to go your own way, I understand."

Justin's lips tightened. He was pissing off his best friend. If only Linc could tell him he wasn't all that happy about it either. When Linc was around Leah, his chest was tight and his heart sped up. She was gorgeous, her innocent beauty tempting him to forget why they could never be together.

"I don't want to go my own damn way. I want to share Leah with you." Justin stood and headed back to the counter. "We're having dinner with Leah tomorrow night. You're going to be nice and charming. We're going to start courting her, dammit. Eventually, I'll find out why you're lying. In the meantime, suck it up, buttercup. Leah's the one. You know it. I know it. And starting tomorrow night, we're going to let Leah know it."

Linc stroked his goatee as Justin strode up to the counter to talk to Josh. Having Leah in his home was a dream come true and a nightmare, all at the same time. He'd fantasized about having her there, cooking in the kitchen, watching the big-screen television while they cuddled on the couch, and of course, making love in his big bed. The more he was with her, the more he wanted to be with her. She was shy and quiet, but her quick, intelligent mind and loving heart shone through.

She's not for me.

He would be friendly and polite tomorrow night, but he wasn't going to court her. Justin could have her. He loved Justin like a brother. If Leah was the one for him, Linc would step aside and let him have her. He wanted them to be happy more than anything.

Linc took a big gulp of the hot liquid, feeling it burn all the way down his throat. He wasn't being a selfless hero giving Leah up to Justin.

Linc was protecting himself.

Chapter Two

Leah fiddled with the napkin, trying not to feel out of place among the four other women. She was having dinner with Cassie, Jillian, Becca, and Ava at the diner, and as usual she didn't know what to say. She wasn't good in a group.

Jillian placed a comforting hand on her arm. Leah knew Jillian the best of all three women. She was a fiery redhead with two handsome husbands, Sheriff Ryan Parks and his brother Jack, a firefighter. "I dragged Leah here kicking and screaming. I was at the bookstore when Justin Reynolds asked her to have dinner with him and Linc tomorrow night."

Instead of expressions of amazement, the other women's eyes lit up with enthusiasm.

"Aren't you surprised he asked me out? I am. I'm not exactly his type."

Becca Miller smiled. The petite, pretty blonde owned the local hair salon and was married to a doctor and a lawyer. "I think that's exactly the point. Justin and Linc could have any of those women who are their so-called type. Those women come to them. If it's one thing I've learned...it's that men like to strive for things. If something comes to them too easily, they don't value it."

Ava Bryant nodded in agreement. She had long dark hair and sparkling green eyes. She was recently engaged to three hunky men in town who owned the coffee shop and the martial arts studio. "Becca's right. Men like to play sports, take over companies, compete. It gets their adrenaline going, and when their adrenaline is engaged, it engages their emotions."

Leah frowned. "What does that have to do with me? Are you trying to say I should play hard to get?"

"Fuck no." Jillian laughed. "You shouldn't play hard to get, you should *be* hard to get. Make sure they treat you with respect at all times. Don't take any crap. Don't let them get away with any bad-boy behavior. Those other women probably let those boys do whatever they wanted. You let Justin and Linc know they have to treat you like a lady and court you. They'll come running."

Cassie Harper pointed to Jillian. Cassie was a tiny, delicate blonde with bright blue eyes. She was married to local businessmen Zach and Chase Harper. "Jillian knows what she's talking about. She had to lay down the law with Jack. He straightened up right quick. Now he's a model husband."

Becca rolled her eyes. "Let's not go that far. Model? Shit, he's still my brother. How about he doesn't drive Jillian crazy anymore?"

Leah slumped in her chair. "I can't imagine Justin Reynolds and Linc Davis running after me. Especially not Linc. Didn't you tell them?"

Jillian shook her head. "No, it wasn't my place to say. Maybe we heard what he said out of context?"

Cassie sipped her iced tea. "What did Linc say?"

Leah looked away. The words were still painful. "He said he wasn't interested in me. He said I wasn't his type, and he didn't want to have dinner with me." She looked back at Jillian. "And I don't think we heard him out of context. He said what he said. I need to just get over it."

Becca's face was red with anger. "That asshole. Justin is a total sweetie, Leah. What you see is what you get. Linc, well, Linc is sweet, too, but much more complex. There's always something simmering just below the surface, you know what I mean? The whole still-waters thing." She took a drink of her tea and slammed the glass down on the table with a thump. "I'm going to kick his ass next time I see him."

Leah shook her head. "No, you're not. He can't help what he feels. He didn't know I'd overhear him. He wasn't trying to be mean. He was being honest."

Cassie's blue eyes were soft. "What did he say when he found out you overheard him?"

"He didn't find out. Jillian and I went over to the counter. He doesn't need to know I know. I want to have some pride left."

Ava frowned. "So, let me get this straight. You're going to have dinner tomorrow night with two sexy men. One of them wants you there, and one of them doesn't. They think you think they both want you there. In actuality, you know only one wants you there. Whew! A tangled web, Leah. How are you going to play it then?"

Jillian slapped the table. "That's why I brought Leah here tonight. We need to help her through this. I'm trying to convince her to let us make her over a little. Make Linc realize he's passing up something he shouldn't."

Becca's eyes sparkled and she started bouncing up and down in her seat. "A makeover? Can we? I'd love to get my hands on your hair, Leah. It's so gorgeous. It just needs a few layers and some thinning."

Cassie grinned. "And some brighter colors. You have a cute figure, but you hide it under those earth tones and prim blouses. I think we're about the same size. I could lend you something. After all, I won't be wearing most of my wardrobe for a while." She patted her still-flat stomach. She was three months pregnant and glowing.

Leah grabbed a handful of strands. "My hair is a mop. I can't do anything with it so I just leave it loose."

Becca patted her hand. "Leave it to me. I know just what to do to make your fabulous hair even more fabulous."

Could she do this? Did she even want to do this? She'd always said a man had to want her for herself.

A new haircut and a new outfit wouldn't change who she was inside. It was a minor thing and she did want to look her best, not only for her date, but in general. It was time she stopped blending into the background.

She nodded. "Okay, I'll do it."

Ava laughed. "Good for you. Give 'em hell. Let them know who's in charge."

Becca picked up her fork as their meals were delivered. "We'll head to the salon right after dinner. I'll call Mark and Travis and have them bring Noah there so I can nurse him."

Becca's brand-new baby son was so precious and Mark and Travis were strutting around town, completely proud dads. It was cute to watch. Leah wondered if she'd ever be lucky enough to find a man as loving and caring as those two.

Jillian dug into her mashed potatoes. "See, I told you this would be a good thing. You should come to dinner with us every week. I've been inviting you forever, and I'm glad you finally came."

Leah was glad she came, too. It was time to come out of her shell and live a little. Tonight was only the first step.

* * * *

Justin chopped the celery and scraped it from the cutting board into the salad bowl. He was prepping food for dinner tonight with Leah. He wanted to get as much of the grunt work out of the way before she arrived.

Linc entered the kitchen in workout shorts and a towel slung over his shoulders.

"Dressed a little casually for guests, aren't you?"

Linc rubbed the towel over his sweaty face and scowled. "I don't have a guest coming over. You do."

"Don't you make a damn face at me. I don't know what your deal is but I do know you're a lying sack of crap. Eventually, I'll get it out of you, but for tonight you need to get your ass upstairs, take a shower, dress decently, and then make Leah feel at home and welcome. Anything less would be rude. Do you want to hurt Leah's feelings? She's a sensitive woman. She didn't appreciate your crack at the bookstore about baking cupcakes."

His friend had the grace to look ashamed. "I didn't mean it the way it came out. I think it's really nice she's so sweet and old-fashioned."

"Don't be an asshole tonight. I know you like her. Act like it."

Linc turned away and grabbed a bottle of water from the refrigerator. "Leah's a nice woman but she's not going to be my woman."

Justin took a deep breath, trying not to lose his patience with the man he loved like a brother. Linc was the reason Justin had even had a career in music.

"I know you want her. Why are you fighting it?" A thought came to Justin's mind. "Do you think she's a virgin or something? Shit, Linc, she's twenty-seven. She's surely had sex."

Linc downed half the bottle of water in one long drink before answering. "No, I don't think she's a virgin, but I also don't think she's got a hell of a lot of experience. She blushes every five seconds."

Justin grinned. "She's beautiful when she blushes."

Linc started to nod in agreement, but quickly stopped and stared into the refrigerator as if there was something fascinating in there. Justin didn't know why but Linc appeared to have his head up his ass. A very long way. It was up to Justin to make sure he didn't do something stupid he would regret later.

Justin walked over and pushed the refrigerator door shut and got into Linc's face. "I'm serious. Don't be an asshole. Be sweet to Leah. We've spent too much time trying to get her comfortable enough to go out with us." Justin was only getting warmed up. He had much more to say on the subject of Linc's stubbornness, but Linc's cell phone interrupted him before he could get going again.

Justin smiled. Linc's ring tone was Justin's biggest hit,

"Affirmative Love." That single had gone triple platinum.

"Are you done lecturing me? Am I allowed to answer the phone or will that upset Leah, too?"

Linc's jaw was tight, but Justin didn't give a damn. Their years of friendship gave him the right to give Linc hell whenever he wanted to.

"If it did hurt Leah's feelings, my answer would be no. Answer the fucking phone then, if you're too chickenshit to tell me what your issue is with Leah."

Linc looked ready to slug him, but grabbed his phone off the kitchen counter instead.

"Hello."

Linc's features relaxed immediately. "Bobbi, we haven't heard from you in almost a year."

Linc pressed the speaker button on his phone and set it on the table between them. They both knew Bobbi from way back in the day. She was a good concert promoter, and although not really a friend, she would definitely be considered a close acquaintance.

"Hey, Linc. How's Florida? Getting a tan?"

Linc chuckled. "It's February and about fifty degrees. Not exactly beach weather. How's that new husband of yours? Still in newlywed heaven I bet?"

There was a moment of silence before she answered. "Married life is more than I ever thought. It's been eight months of bliss. Listen, is Justin there, too?"

"I'm right here," Justin said.

"Hey, Justin. How are the golden pipes? Have you written anything lately?"

Justin rolled his eyes. No one ever asked him about anything but his voice and his music. He had other interests, not that anyone cared.

"The pipes are fine, and no, I haven't really written anything. Too busy these days."

"Too bad. I was thinking you might want to show off some new material. I'm putting together a concert tour. I want to do something really special. It's going to be a group of rock bands, at least four or five. Huge venues. It'll be like Woodstock but every week a new concert."

Linc was immediately in business mode.

"What time frame? What bands were you planning to have? Is this an American tour or European?"

"A summer tour. America with the final show here in New York. Madison Square Garden, of course. As for the bands, I've got tentative agreement from the Loggers, Crime Hearts, and Safety Sign."

Justin and Linc exchanged puzzled looks. All those bands had split up and retired years ago. Linc looked at Justin and hit the Mute button on the phone.

Justin shook his head. "No way. I'm retired."

Linc nodded and unmuted the phone. "Listen, Bobbi. Justin retired from touring. Fuck, we're both too old for the grind of traveling from city to city. He might do an album every three or four years, but he's decided to not tour or promote. Any sales will just be on word of mouth."

"That's not a very efficient way to sell albums. Shit, the Rolling Stones still tour and they're like a hundred years old. You're not even forty."

Justin didn't like Bobbi's nasty tone. She was usually very professional.

Justin pulled the phone closer to him. "I'm not Mick Jagger. Never pretended to be, either. It's very sweet of you to think about us and give us this chance, Bobbi. But I'm retired. I like retirement. I have no desire to tour, ever again. It was great to hear from you, though. Glad to hear you're a happy newlywed."

"Think about it." Bobbi's tone was cool and clipped. She obviously was surprised they'd turned her down. "This is a big opportunity. I'll call you in a few days after you've had time to mull it over."

"We won't change our minds," Linc answered. "Justin's retired. We're done. But I also want to say thanks for offering this to us. It was good of you, Bobbi."

"I'll call again in a few days. Don't be a fucking idiot, Justin. Do you want to be a has-been?"

The call was disconnected and Justin was left shaking his head in disbelief.

"A has-been, huh? I can only hope. That's why we moved to a small town. They don't give a flying rat's ass if I was a rock star or president of the United States. She's in a bitchy mood today. Never heard her speak like that, have you?"

Linc tapped the phone on the kitchen table. "Bobbi's always been intense, but she's also always been a consummate professional. She always talked about how people can be nasty about women in business, calling them bitches and such. She was careful to project a certain image."

"Let's face it. In the music business, image is everything."

Justin should know. His image as the squeaky-clean, all-American golden boy of rock was legendary. It had propelled him to the top of the heap of singers and songwriters who probably had more talent but didn't have Linc to manage their careers.

Linc tossed the phone on to the counter. "Well, I hope Bobbi finds another band. It sounds like an ambitious idea. Woodstock every week during the summer?" He laughed. "She'll need an army to pull it off. The logistics will be a nightmare. Not to mention she'll need some generous sponsors to front the money. It'll be expensive as hell."

Justin shrugged. "I wish her the best of luck. She's a good promoter." He looked at his watch and jumped up from the table. "Leah's going to be here in about an hour. You need to get in the shower. I need to keep working on dinner. Remember what I said. Don't be an asshole and scare her off."

Linc started for the stairs. "I'll be nice, but I'm not romancing her.

You are."

Justin watched Linc head up the stairs. Linc was hiding something from him, and he was damn sure going to find out what it was. Something was keeping Linc from being with Leah. He knew Linc as well as he knew himself. Linc was attracted to Leah, as much or more than he was. Tonight, Justin was going to make sure Leah understood she'd have to want both of them.

No matter what Linc said, Justin knew he wanted her.

* * * *

"I'll be right there!"

Leah was putting the finishing touches on her lip gloss when she heard the peal of the doorbell. She gave herself one last look in the mirror. Becca had done an amazing job on her hair. The change was subtle but made styling her thick, heavy hair a breeze. She was also wearing an outfit borrowed from Cassie's seemingly massive wardrobe. The skinny jeans seemed to make her legs look longer and the pink cashmere wraparound sweater made her waist look tiny. The outfit was topped off with high-heeled, chocolate-brown suede boots from Ava. Ava was about the same height as Leah and wore high heels quite a bit. Leah had never seen the point but had to admit she liked the confidence they gave her.

The doorbell rang again, the person pushing the button over and over again for fun now. She heaved a sigh of exasperation. It was probably someone coming to save her soul or get her to vote for their candidate.

"Coming!"

She pulled open the door and stared straight into a broad, muscled chest in uniform. She had to look up to see his face. She smiled with delight.

"Jason, I didn't know you were going to stop by. Aren't you on duty tonight?"

Her cousin, Jason Carrington, was a deputy on the Plenty police force. They were as close as brother and sister, at home with each other, having grown up together. Jason was funny and easy to be around, making her laugh and enjoying her chocolate-chip cookies.

"I am. I'm on a quick break though."

Leah stepped back and checked her watch. She needed to talk to Jason but didn't want to be late for dinner with Justin and Linc.

"You checked your watch. Are you heading somewhere?"

She put her hands on her hips in disgust. Men were so dense sometimes.

"Look at me, Jase. Do I look like I'm ready for an evening in front of the television? I have plans, if you must know."

No use trying to keep anything a secret from her cousin. He seemed to know everyone's secrets, and most especially hers. He could read expressions in a heartbeat.

Jason pursed his lips, looking her up and down. "As a matter of fact, you do seem a little dressed up. Who's the lucky guy?"

Leah smoothed the sweater over her hips. "None of your business."

He was going to find out, but she didn't need to make it easy for him. Teasing Jason was something she enjoyed.

He headed straight back to the kitchen with a snort. "I'm not falling for it, cuz. You want to yank my chain. No way. You'll tell me eventually. You always do. Now where are you hiding the cookies? I'm starved."

He found the cookie jar on top of the fridge and grinned. "Eureka. Cookies." His smile fell as quickly as it had come. "Oatmeal? Damn, I was hoping for chocolate chip."

"I can't make chocolate chip every time. I was in the mood for oatmeal this week."

He grabbed five cookies. "I'll only take a few then. So what did you need to talk to me about? I got your message but wasn't able to get here until now. I was fishing out at the lake today and turned off my cell."

"That's a few, huh? Good thing I made six dozen." Her voice softened. "Why don't you sit down and I'll get you a glass of iced tea. We need to talk."

She poured Jason a glass as he settled himself at the table. This was going to be a tough discussion. She looked at her watch again. Luckily, she took so little time getting ready she shouldn't be late for dinner.

She sat across from Jason and grabbed his hand. "Gabe called me. He's coming home."

She let Jason absorb her words. He was quiet for a long time before speaking.

"Is he okay?"

His voice was even, but she could hear the emotion underneath. Despite being cousins, Gabe and Jason were as close as brothers. They'd intended to share a woman at one point in their lives. Iraq had changed everything. Jason came back with minor physical and mental scars. Gabe was a different story. She loved her brother, but she couldn't understand what had kept him away from the people who cared about him this long.

"He's okay. He had an accident on his motorcycle. Nothing serious, but he hurt his leg. He's coming home, Jason."

Jason sat back, his expression neutral. "Just passing through or for good?"

She blinked rapidly, trying not to shed tears. She hadn't seen Gabe for over two years. "I was afraid to ask, honestly. He asked if he could stay with me and I said yes, of course. We'll have to make everything so wonderful for him he won't ever want to leave again."

She could see the hurt in Jason's eyes. Gabe hadn't called him or asked to stay with him. Five years ago it would have been unthinkable. They'd been practically inseparable. Leah had been the outsider, always jealous of the special bond they shared. Now she would have to be the mediator between the two.

Jason took a gulp of the tea. "I'm sure you will, cuz. Sounds like my presence won't be needed, though."

She squeezed Jason's hand, begging him to understand. "Gabe's going to need us both. I know he's different now, but we can't give up hope."

The corner of Jason's mouth tipped up. "Hope? I've always had hope. There hasn't been a fucking day that's gone by since I got back from the Middle East that I haven't thought about Gabe. I feel incomplete when he's not here. But he's changed, Leah. Those few months he was home, he was a different man. An angry man, out of control."

Leah nodded. She couldn't deny how bitter and mean Gabe had become. It was awful to say, but she and Jason had been a little relieved when he'd left town. They simply hadn't known how to help him. They also never thought he'd stay away so long.

"I know you miss Samantha, too," Leah whispered, watching Jason's expression become tortured.

"Samantha did what she had to do. In her place, I don't know that I'd have done anything different." Jason stood up and placed his glass in the sink. "When will he be here?"

"In a few days. I'll have him call you as soon as he's here."

Jason rubbed his chin with is hand. "You do that. Pardon me if I don't wait by the phone. Gabe hasn't called me in all this time, so I'm guessing we don't have much left to say. I'm glad he's kept in touch with you, though."

Leah wasn't sure she'd call a phone call or an e-mail every few months "keeping in touch," but it was more than Jason had ever received.

"Don't you have something to say to him? You deserve the chance to be heard, too."

Jason pulled her in for a hug. "You're a good girl, Leah Holt. Whoever is getting to take you out tonight is a lucky man. Chances are, you're too good for him."

"I'm having dinner with Justin Reynolds and Linc Davis."

She closed her eyes, waiting for the explosion. When it didn't come, she opened one eye a little to peek up at her cousin. He was shaking his head.

"Not good enough for you, cuz. I know he's a former rock star and has women throwing themselves at him, but those guys? Guys from the big city? Why can't you date a couple of nice guys from Plenty?"

She rolled her eyes. "Because none of those guys ask me out. Justin and Linc did. They're making me dinner tonight."

Jason cleared his throat. "Well, be careful. They seem nice enough, but those city boys move at a faster pace." He dug into his wallet and pulled out a strip of condoms. "You better take these. Just in case."

She pressed her hands to her face in sheer mortification. "Dear God, Jason, put those away. It's only dinner. And if you're carrying those, what pace do you move at?"

Jason chuckled at her predicament. "Whatever pace pleases the lady I'm with. Take them." He pressed them in her hand. "There's nothing shameful about sex or having sex. It's pretty great, if you ask me."

"I've had sex before."

"Then you know that sexual attraction is a strong, powerful thing and you shouldn't be caught unprepared. Do you have any questions about ménage sex?"

She wanted the kitchen floor to open up and swallow her. "Where is the Angel of Death when I need him?" She pointed to the door. "Get out. Take your cookies and go before you say something that's going to make it really uncomfortable to have Thanksgiving dinner with you."

Jason grabbed three more cookies and headed for the door. Despite her own discomfort, she was glad she'd told him about Justin and Linc. It had pulled him out of his funk regarding Gabe's return.

"Have fun tonight. How about dinner at Charlie's tomorrow night? I'm off duty."

Leah nodded and Jason headed to his SUV. Condoms notwithstanding, her news had gone better than expected. She glanced at her watch and panicked. She had barely enough time to get to Justin and Linc's home. She shoved the condoms in her purse, grabbed the dessert she'd made, and ran out the door. She wasn't going to be late for her date with her dream men. Even if Linc didn't want her, it wouldn't stop her from having a wonderful time with Justin.

She'd be nice and polite to Linc, but nothing else. She had more pride than to throw herself at a man who didn't want her. Even if that man was Linc Davis.

Chapter Three

The house was huge and sprawling. She could probably fit four or five of her condos inside this one house. Her own home was done in the typical Spanish style so popular in Florida, practically interchangeable with every other home. Instead, Justin and Linc had created a more traditional-looking home with a large front porch, with a log and stone facade. Off to the right was another large building with several garage doors. She remembered Justin mentioning he and Linc liked to collect motorcycles. The large lot was lush and green, even now with the dry season, with towering oak and pine trees. It all added up to a homey, inviting atmosphere.

She juggled her purse and the dessert, reaching for the doorbell, and almost dropped everything when the door opened before she had a chance.

"Hey, Leah. Let me help you with that."

Justin took the dessert pan from her and wrapped an arm around her shoulders to lead her in. He must have been watching for her to arrive. The thought that he had been anxious for arrival made her smile.

Justin peered into the pan and grinned. "Wow, is that tiramisu? I love tiramisu and it's Linc's absolute favorite of all time."

She pushed away the feeling of happiness that she had made Linc's favorite anything. She wasn't here for Linc, she was here for Justin.

"It is tiramisu. You mentioned something about Italian so I took a chance and made an Italian dessert."

Justin grinned and led her through the house. She couldn't help gaping in amazement at their home. The ceilings were soaring with exposed beams, the knotty pine floors polished like mirrors. There were large windows everywhere and a huge stone fireplace in the living room. The kitchen was no less impressive with gleaming stainless steel appliances, copper backsplash, and what looked like a wood-fired oven at one end.

She knew she was gawking but she couldn't help it. She'd never seen luxury like this, but the home was clearly set up for comfort.

"Wow, this house is gorgeous. Just beautiful."

Justin grinned. "I'm glad you like it. Linc and I designed it ourselves."

She walked slowly through the kitchen, taking in the all the little touches which made it special.

"I feel like I've been transported out of Florida and to the great Northwest."

Justin looked pleased. "That's what we were going for. Linc and I are from the Seattle area."

"I didn't know that, but it shows. How did you end up in Florida?"

Justin slid the dessert pan into the oversized refrigerator. "How about a glass of wine?"

She nodded and he continued. "Linc and I wanted to move to a ménage town. We did our research and we couldn't find one in the Northwest. There were a few in Texas, one in Colorado, and a couple in the Wyoming and Montana area. We checked them out and they were nice and friendly. We could have lived there easily. When we came to visit Plenty it was different." He poured out a measure of wine and handed her the glass. "It was like the town spoke to us, welcoming us in. Everybody was so nice, the town was charming. We knew it would be a great place to settle down. And no cold winters was a bonus."

Leah sipped the fruity wine, letting it linger on her tongue. It was delicious. "But hot, sticky, humid summers. I'm sure you're not used to that kind of weather."

He lifted the lid on a large pot and stirred, sending the aroma of tomato sauce wafting through the air. Her stomach growled and she pressed a hand to her stomach with a nervous giggle.

Justin laughed. "I promise to feed you very soon. I'm glad you brought an appetite. If there's one thing I hate to see, it's a woman picking at her food. And no, we weren't used to the hot summers, but it wasn't so bad. We learned to try and stay indoors during midday or at least be in the pool."

Leah stepped closer to the windows. "You have a pool? The condo association I live in has a pool, but I have to share it with everyone else."

Justin pulled a cast iron skillet from the oven and replaced it with a sheet of bread with thick butter spread on top. Everything smelled wonderful. If it tasted as good as it smelled, Justin would be the perfect male.

"We do. It's off the family room. We have a whirlpool, too. We can take a soak after dinner if you like."

She felt her face get hot at the thought of seeing Justin and Linc in nothing but a swimsuit. "I didn't bring a suit."

Justin chuckled. "Do you need one? We won't look."

"We won't look at what?" Linc strolled in looking devastatingly handsome in blue jeans and a white button-down shirt. He had a rakish air with his dark hair, dark eyes, and goatee.

Justin started pouring Linc a glass of wine. "Leah. I was telling her we had a whirlpool and she said she didn't bring a suit. I was saying we wouldn't look."

Linc arched an eyebrow. "You're a real boy scout. Don't believe a word he says, Leah. He would definitely look."

Would you?

She bit her lip so she wouldn't ask the question that was hanging in the air. Of course Linc wouldn't look. She wasn't his type.

Justin came up behind her and placed his hands on her shoulders. A zing of electricity ran through her body and she breathed in his masculine scent that was mixing with the spicy smell of dinner.

"This woman is hungry. Why don't you take her out to the family room and sit down? We're going to eat at the table in there. I'll bring the food."

She could swear she saw Linc's jaw tighten. "Don't you need help?"

Justin shook his head. "Nope. I'll be right out with the salad. You two get comfortable."

She had no choice but to follow Linc through the kitchen and into the family room. She wasn't sure what family it was meant for, but it was clear men lived in the house. Overstuffed leather furniture faced the largest television she had ever seen. On the far wall a large stone fireplace dominated the room. The other end of the room had several vintage pinball and video game machines, including an air hockey table.

The dining table was set up in front of the crackling fire, complete with candles and a dark-red tablecloth. It was a scene set for romance. She felt her stomach flutter and her palms start to sweat. Everything had been casual and friendly until this moment.

This moment with a man who wasn't interested in her. Justin's interest made her nervous. Linc's indifference made her uncomfortable. She needed to shove those emotions aside and try to relax and enjoy the evening. Whatever was meant to happen would happen. Normally, Leah wasn't one to leave things to fate, but giving the universe the power to control her love life sounded good tonight.

The universe better not screw this up.

* * * *

"Are you ready for dessert?" Leah asked.

They had worked their way through a fresh green salad and Justin's famous chicken parmesan. Now they were relaxing in front of the fireplace, drinking wine. Linc had been hoping he could disappear into his own room soon.

Being around Leah was almost painful. Justin took every opportunity to touch her, brushing her arm, playing with her fingers, even kissing her knuckles when she'd complimented the food.

Linc wanted to touch her creamy, smooth skin. He wanted to kiss her full lips and pull her close to his body, letting the warmth of her scent surround him.

He wasn't going to do it. Instead, he sat very quietly, gripping first his fork, and now his wine glass, so his fingers wouldn't accidentally stray anywhere near her.

"I'm still pretty full. Actually, I need to make a few phone calls. Business."

Linc stood up, trying to make his exit. He hated the pang in his chest when Leah dropped her eyes, looking everywhere but at him. He was a complete and total asshole.

Justin stood, too, helping Leah to her feet. "Business calls on a Tuesday night? Whatever it is can wait until tomorrow. Besides, you're never too full for tiramisu. It's your favorite."

Justin was giving him a look and Linc finally capitulated. The fact was, he really didn't want to be away from Leah, no matter how much it hurt.

Leah's eyes went wide. "I have something in my purse for the dessert. I'll just be a minute."

She dashed toward the foyer, making them both chuckle. She was seriously cute.

Justin was pulling the pan out of the refrigerator when she rejoined them, holding her handbag. She held it up triumphantly.

"I brought birthday candles. You know, so you can make a wish."

Linc knew what he'd wish for. But it wasn't his wish. It was Justin's.

Justin grinned, his eyes soft as he gazed at her. "I know just what I'm going to wish for."

His expression made Leah blush. Linc loved the way the pink

color suffused her cheeks. It made her even more beautiful, if such a thing was possible. She seemed flustered as she shoved her hand in her purse and pulled out the candles. Several items flew out on the kitchen island along with them. Leah froze, her expression turning from embarrassment to horror. Finally, Linc saw the instrument of her mortification.

A strip of condoms. Lubricated with a reservoir tip.

Linc felt sorry for her and tried to break the tension with a joke. "It appears you already knew Justin's wish. Smart girl."

* * * *

Leah pressed her hands over her hot face, wishing the earth would open up and swallow her. Justin and Linc looked amused, but this wasn't anything to laugh about. She wanted to hide and never see them again, but in a town the size of Plenty it wasn't going to happen.

"I–I can explain. At least, I think I can. You see, my cousin Jason came over and well, I–I told him I was coming here, and he said how fast city men were, and well, oh hell."

She broke off, realizing she had probably made things even worse. She'd basically insulted them, calling them man whores.

Way to go.

She pressed her lips together and tried to think of something, anything, to say at a moment such as this. She sighed.

"It was all Jason's idea."

The men looked perfectly serious and then doubled over in laughter. Even Linc, who was normally reserved, had a red face from laughing. Finally, he took a deep breath and tried to look calm, but his lips were twitching.

"Honey, it sounds like Jason was being cautious. This wouldn't happen to be Deputy Jason, would it?"

She nodded. "He's my cousin. Since my parents died, he's been very protective of me." Now wasn't the time to talk about her brother,

Gabe, and the family dynamics with Jason and his sisters.

Justin shook his head. "Remind me not to get stopped for speeding. I'll never keep a straight face." He grabbed her hand. "It's okay, sweetheart. Linc and I have a good sense of humor, and your cousin was only doing what he thought was right. He doesn't know us very well, so we can see why he might be cautious about you getting involved with us."

It was a relief they understood. She twisted the candle box between her nervous fingers. Being this close to them was exhausting. She had to hold back her natural instinct to move even closer, run her hands over their bodies, and smell their yummy scent. "Are we getting involved?"

Justin plucked the birthday candles from her hand. "Yes. Let's get these lit so I can make my wish."

He stuck a couple of candles in the dessert and Linc lit them. Justin leaned down to blow them out, closing his eyes. "My wish better come true." He easily blew both of them out with one breath. His grin was gleeful. "I get my wish."

Leah laughed at his boyish expression. "What did you wish for?"

She gasped as he pulled her close to his body. "I wished for this."

His hands ran down her back and his lips gently caressed hers. She could barely breathe, lost in the sensations of actually being this close to Justin. His citrus scent teased her nostrils and a few strands of his shaggy bangs brushed the oversensitized skin of her face. Her hands clutched his shoulders, digging into the muscles and feeling the heat radiate from his body.

His tongue was playing sensuous games in her mouth and his fingers were tangling in her hair, angling her head exactly where he wanted it. He tasted of spices and wine and something she'd never tasted before but was instantly addictive. Her body was responding, her nipples tingling and her pussy getting damp.

She was breathing heavy when he finally lifted his head, his expression stamped with arousal. It was a heady feeling to know he was as affected as she. She looked over at Linc, who was watching them with an inscrutable expression. One flicker of a glance at his crotch told her he wasn't unaffected. He was aroused watching her kiss Justin, even if he wasn't attracted to her himself.

Linc was close enough she could reach her hand out and touch him, but at the moment he seemed a million miles away. Justin turned her toward Linc as if to indicate she should kiss him, too. Linc never moved, his body stiff, frozen in place.

She looked back at Justin and he gave her a smile of encouragement. She looked back at Linc. He still hadn't moved, hadn't changed his expression. There was no passion or tenderness to be found, only a man turned to stone. Her body instantly went from hot and aroused to cold and bleak. He didn't want her and it made her heart squeeze in her chest painfully. She couldn't stand the way he was looking at her. She turned back to Justin and pressed herself against his body, trying to feel warm again. She pulled his head down for another kiss, determined Linc's indifference wouldn't ruin her night with Justin.

She could feel her heart breaking as Linc finally moved, leaving them alone. Justin turned and started to pull away to follow him, but she held on to his arm.

"Let him go. He doesn't want me. It's okay."

Justin shook his head, his color high. "Yes, he does. He wants you as much as I do."

Leah blinked back the tears that were starting to sting the back of her eyes. "I don't want there to be any lies between us. I know the truth. I heard Linc saying he wasn't attracted to me when you were in the bookstore yesterday. If you want me, it's enough."

It was more than she ever thought she would have.

Justin's jaw tightened as he looked where his friend had exited the room. "I do want you. Dammit, Leah, he does, too. He's just scared of something. I don't know what it is, but I'll be damned if I let him hurt you."

She caressed Justin's jaw, turning his face back to her. "He didn't hurt me."

He closed his eyes in frustration. "He did hurt you. I can see it, hell, I could feel it."

She leaned close to him, placing her head on his chest, feeling the rise and fall of his chest and hearing the steady thump of his heartbeat.

"Okay, he hurt me. I doubt he meant to. Linc doesn't seem cruel. He's a nice man who isn't into me. That's all."

Justin stroked her hair. "He is into you. Leah, we're both crazy about you. I see the way he looks at you. Fuck, I know how I look at you. I've been taking it slow for a long time to let you get used to us. I can't wait anymore. I want you, baby. I want to take you upstairs and make love to you. Will you let me do that? Will you let us?"

Leah pulled back and looked into his beautiful blue eyes, dark with passion. She'd been playing it safe her entire life. Something rare and precious was in her grasp. She was going to hold on to it as long as it would last.

"Linc doesn't want me, but if you do? Yes, let's go upstairs."

Chapter Four

Justin vacillated between being furious with Linc and ecstatic at Leah's positive reaction to his declaration of desire. Part of him wanted to go pound some sense into Linc's head and kick his ass. The other part wanted to sweep Leah off her feet and carry her upstairs to his bedroom. The latter part won.

He couldn't force Linc to make love to Leah, but he wasn't going to pass up his opportunity. Linc had feelings for Leah, and watching Justin make love to her without joining in was going to be impossible. Justin was sure Linc would join them in the bedroom eventually.

In the meantime, he was going to show her all the pleasure he could bring her. As he carried her up the stairs, she felt perfect in his arms. Her slight weight was no burden, and he nuzzled her neck, breathing in her sweet scent. She even giggled when he nipped at the soft skin, kicking her feet in delight. He set her gently down on the bed and started pulling off her suede boots.

"Wait!" She held up her hand, her cheeks pink. "Um, aren't we going to kiss or something first?"

He tossed first one boot, then the other, over his shoulder. "We are definitely going to kiss and 'or something' first. I just thought we should be comfortable when we do. Aren't you warm in that sweater?"

He slid his hands under the soft cashmere knit to the silky, warm flesh underneath. He felt her tremble under his hands and his cock responded, pressing insistently against his zipper.

She licked her lips. "A little. Aren't you warm, too?"

He grinned. His shy girl had a bold streak. He was happy to

indulge it. "I am warm, now that you mention it. Must be the company heating my blood." He stripped off his shirt and tossed it aside while she giggled. It was the sweetest sound he'd ever heard.

He loved the way her soft brown eyes opened a little wider and the pupils dilated as she let her gaze roam over his bare chest. Both he and Linc worked out five days a week and he was proud of being in good shape. He wanted this woman to find pleasure in looking at him. He stood and popped the button on his blue jeans. She seemed to hold her breath as he lowered his zipper slowly before kicking them away. His black boxers were tented with his erection, but it felt good to be free of the pants' restriction.

She was looking him up and down, making his cock swell and the blood pump through his veins. He needed to dial it down. He wanted to take this first time slow.

He was shocked when she reached out and ran her hands up his thighs and cupped his hard dick through the thin material. He groaned at the feel of her fingers caressing him. He grabbed her wrists.

"Easy, honey. I want to take this slow, and I'm so excited, if you keep that up, this will be over before it starts."

His sweet, shy woman was a surprise in the bedroom. She dropped to her knees and looked up at him with an expression he was sure Eve used in the Garden of Eden.

"I can help you with that, if you like."

She was looking up at him through her impossibly long lashes and giving him a shy smile. His cock was clamoring for attention, and she leaned forward and rubbed her cheek against him, sending flashes of lightning up his cock and straight to his balls.

He jumped back, trying to keep control. "Holy shit. Fuck."

He stepped closer again, his hand curving behind her neck. He wasn't capable of saying no at this moment to her generous offer. "Are you sure, honey? You don't have to do this."

She smiled and tugged at his boxers. "I want to. I don't think I'm very good at it, but I really want you in my mouth. Is that okay?"

Okay? Fuck, yeah.

"It's always okay, honey. You can have me in your mouth anytime you want. I'm sure you're fine at this. There's no right or wrong way, just don't bite down. That would hurt."

He helped her pull his boxers all the way down and his cock sprang free. She immediately gave it a lick from balls to tip, and a moan was ripped from his throat at the rush of pleasure. Her tongue was warm and wet, and he wasn't going to last long.

She wrapped her hand around the base of his cock and started lapping at the head, already dripping his pre-cum. He wound his fingers into her thick, silky hair.

"Suck me."

* * * *

Leah swirled her tongue around the head of Justin's cock, the taste of him exploding on her tongue. She hummed in pleasure before engulfing as much of him as she could. He was so large she could only go about halfway down the thick shaft before he bumped the back of her throat. She flicked her tongue on the sensitive underside and began an up-and-down motion she hoped would send him over the edge. She wanted to make him feel amazing.

She hadn't done this very often, but one look at his tortured expression let her know he was enjoying it. She wrapped one hand around the base of his cock and placed the other on his hard, muscled thighs. She could feel the quiver underneath her palm and knew he was close. His breathing was heavy and his eyes were closed in ecstasy.

She paused for a moment, thinking she had seen movement out of the corner of her eye. Justin's strong hands caressed her hair.

"Are you okay, honey?"

She nodded and took him slightly deeper, relaxing her jaw a little more. She must be imagining things. It was probably just a bird outside the window casting a shadow.

His breath came out in a hiss and his fingers tightened on the back of her head.

"Pull off, honey. I'm going to come in a minute."

She tightened her hand around him and sped up her efforts. He groaned and threw back his head, biting off a filthy word.

She let her other hand trail to his balls, her nails scraping softly against the crinkly skin. He froze, his hand on the back of her head. His cock seemed to swell inside her mouth and then he was shooting his hot seed into the back of her throat. She swallowed down the salty, musky liquid and then sat back on her heels. Justin's fingers loosened and his breathing was ragged. He finally looked down at her with a scowl.

"I told you to pull off. You got a mouthful."

She giggled. "Technically, I already had a mouthful. More than a mouthful."

He finally gave her a lopsided grin. "I guess you did. Are you okay? Do you need a glass of water or something?"

She pressed a kiss to the tip of his cock. "I'm fine." She rubbed his thighs with her hands. "In fact, I've never been better." She felt wonderful, her usual shyness not a factor at the moment. She could see the desire in Justin's eyes. She hoped he could see the same thing reflected in hers.

He reached down and pulled her to her feet, kissing her long and hard on the mouth.

"I can see you're the naughty kind. I might have to turn you over my knee if you continue to disobey me."

She felt a gush of honey from her pussy at his threat. The thought of being bent over his lap and his hand punishing her ass was an erotic one. He laughed.

"I can see the thought arouses you. Your eyes are sparkling, your breath sped up, and your skin is flushed. If you want a spanking, I'm your man. I love to spank a disobedient woman. Linc does, too."

She didn't want to think about Linc right now. It was too painful. Instead, she decided to tease Justin. She ran a fingernail around a flat male nipple, watching it tighten in reaction. She was surprised to see his nipples were sensitive.

"I wasn't disobedient. Even if I was, I don't have to do what you say. It's a free country. I'll do whatever I want to."

He chuckled at her bravado. "It is a free country. Everywhere but in the bedroom, honey. When it comes to sex, Linc and I are in charge. We rule the roost, so to speak. You'll do as you're told, and like it."

She did like it. Her nipples were poking holes in her sweater she was so turned on. She was shocked she liked his caveman tactics, but had read enough to know it wasn't uncommon for someone to enjoy giving up control in the bedroom. She wasn't going to give in easily, though.

"I'm not sure how I feel about this. Are you saying I'm some sort of sex slave?"

She was smiling so he would know she wasn't upset. He tilted her chin up so she was looking him in the eye. "A slave to the pleasure. In a few minutes you're going to want to come so badly you'll promise me anything and everything. I can keep you on the edge of release until you understand who holds the reins when it comes to sex."

She hadn't had much luck with orgasms. "I doubt what you say is true. I'm not that easy, Justin."

His eyebrow quirked up. "Is that a challenge?"

She shrugged her shoulders. "If you want it to be. I don't have orgasms easily, just so you know. I doubt there'll be any begging from me."

Justin grinned. "I'm sorry to hear you've had trouble in the past. If anything, it's going to make my job easier, though. I can't wait to give you pleasure like you've never experienced before." He tugged at her sweater. "Let's get you out of these clothes and on that bed. The challenge starts now."

Justin stripped her quickly and efficiently. Before she knew it, she was standing in front of him without a stitch of clothes. She tried to cross her arms over her small breasts but he wasn't having any of it. He brushed her arms back to her sides.

"Don't you dare cover your gorgeous body. I want to see all of it."

She struggled to keep her hands by her side. "I don't have a voluptuous body like the women I've seen you with."

He kissed her hard, nipping her bottom lip. "You must have a really low opinion of me."

She shook her head, shocked to hear him say those words. If anything, the opposite was true.

"I don't."

He tilted his head. "Are you sure? You seem to think I only care about how you look. You seem to think I only find one type of woman sexy and beautiful."

When he said it that way, it made her feel silly. If he was a shallow man, she wouldn't be interested in him in the least. It was all the wonderful things about him which made him attractive.

"You're right. I'm sorry. I guess I've always been self-conscious about my small breasts."

He cupped her breasts and teased the nipples with his thumbs. "They're perfect, just right for my hands. Your body is sexy, Leah. But do you know what I find most sexy about you?"

His hands were doing naughty things to her nipples and she was finding it hard to concentrate on his question.

"Um, no."

He leaned forward and brushed her ear with his lips. "Your mind. Your mind is sexy. You're smart, and funny, and inquisitive, with a zest for life I admire. Sex starts in the brain, you know. How many times have you pictured us together like this? I know I have about a million times. It makes me hard every time. Does it make you wet?"

She licked her lips and nodded, past any sort of verbal ability. He was right. Sex started in the brain, and he'd wormed his way into hers. His warm hands ran all over her body, finding all the sensitive spots and making her crazy. Her knees were ready to give out when he lifted her and placed her gently on the bed.

He covered her body with his own, pressing kisses on her face, neck, ears, and lips. She could feel the heat of his body and the roughness of the hair on his legs and arms in contrast to the silky hair on his chest. She ran her fingers through it, loving the feel of it against her skin. His cock was hard again already and pressed between them. She hooked her leg around his and pulled him closer, hungering to feel him inside of her. Her pussy clenched, feeling empty and needy.

Justin pulled back, reached into the nightstand, and pulled out his phone with a smile. "Here's the challenge. I'm going to set the timer on my phone. If I can't make you come in the next fifteen minutes, you get to be in charge in the bedroom. However, if I make you come before the alarm goes off, I'm in charge. Deal?"

Fifteen minutes didn't seem like enough time. The few lovers she'd had rarely made her come in an entire evening. What if she couldn't come in the time allotted? The fact was she really didn't want to be in charge. Hell, she wouldn't know what to do if she was. She had no desire to spank Justin. The idea was ludicrous and not a turn-on at all.

The doubt must have shown on her face. "You don't think I can do it? Honey, I'm going to send you into orbit tonight. More than once."

Damn, he was arrogant. She loved his self-confidence, but at the moment it was annoying. This was her body he was talking about. If he couldn't make her come, and she ended up in charge, she could always order him to be in charge, right?

"Fine," she snapped. "Deal."

Geez, men are so competitive. Becca was right.

Justin set the alarm and started trailing wet kisses down her neck, cheek, and to her abdomen. She squirmed as he nibbled at her rib cage and then licked her belly button. He kissed a path back to her breasts and ran his tongue around each nipple, watching as they tightened into hard nubs. He drew one into his mouth, sucking until she moaned underneath him, while his fingers plucked at the other, her honey dripping from her pussy. She was more turned on than she'd ever been and he'd only just begun. He still had more than ten minutes on the clock.

He ran his tongue lazily from the valley between her breasts to her already drenched pussy. He pushed her thighs apart, insinuating himself so his mouth hovered over her cunt. She could feel his hot breath on her clit and she shuddered with arousal. She wanted his mouth on her more than she had ever wanted anything, but she didn't want him doing something out of obligation. She pushed at his broad shoulders.

"You don't have to just because I did."

He licked at her inner thigh and gave her an evil smile. "Good, because I'm not. Listen to me, Leah. I'm going to lick your pretty pink pussy because I want to. I want your honey on my tongue and your clit in my mouth. I want to shove my tongue inside you and fuck you with it. Am I being clear?"

She swallowed hard, a flush sweeping through her body at his plain speech. Her voice came out as a hoarse whisper. "Very clear."

When his mouth came down on her, the ability to speak fled. She closed her eyes and let the pleasure wash over her. Justin was right. He was sending her into orbit and this was more than she'd ever experienced. His tongue was tracing the folds of her cunt and circling her swollen nub. Her head was thrashing back and forth and she knew release was a hair's breadth away. She would promise him anything if only he would help her find that elusive orgasm. She was so close.

He closed his lips over clit, scraping it lightly with his teeth, and then sucking on it. She screamed his name as the climax hit her. It was like being broadsided by a freight train. Her body shook and the waves of pleasure were relentless. She was held in their thrall until finally she came down, being held close in Justin's arms.

She faintly heard the chirping of the alarm and Justin reaching to turn it off before folding her close to his heart. She nuzzled his chest, listening to the steady beat of his heart.

Eventually, she started to squirm, her body still unsatisfied. She needed to feel his hard cock inside her, thrusting hard and fast. She encircled him with her fingers and heard his indrawn breath.

"Witch. I was trying to give you a chance to catch your breath."

She caressed him, his cock like velvet steel under her fingers, but pulsing with life. "I don't want to catch my breath. I want you to take my breath away. I want you inside me."

Justin levered himself up and reached into the nightstand again, this time pulling out a condom. She blushed as she remembered how they had ended up in bed in the first place.

Justin grinned. "I know what you're thinking, woman. We would have ended up here anyway, if I'd had my way. I've wanted you for months. I've fantasized about this for months. Sex starts in the brain, remember?"

She did remember, but a moment of insecurity swept through her. "Months? What about all those women that hang around the club?"

She hated herself for asking the question, for being *that* clingy, unsure woman.

Way to drive him away.

His expression didn't turn impatient as she expected. Instead it was incredibly tender. "There are women who hang around. It doesn't mean Linc and I sleep with them. Once I decided on you, I haven't slept with anyone else. For months, honey. I only wanted you."

She wanted to ask about Linc and the two blondes on his arm on Halloween night but didn't want to ruin the moment. After all, Linc owed her nothing. He wasn't in bed with them and hadn't made any promises.

She assumed Justin was so used to sharing women with Linc, he automatically talked about them as if they were here together. He had said he thought Linc would join them, but so far, he hadn't. It was just as well. She didn't need the emotional complication of Linc at the moment.

She nodded. "Thank you for telling me. I'm sorry I asked to begin with. You don't owe me any explanations for anything that may have happened before tonight."

Justin ripped open the condom wrapper. "Don't sell yourself short. You have the right to demand that Linc and I toe the line. Don't put up with any crap behavior from us." He rolled on the condom and tossed the wrapper on the nightstand. "I'll admit I've been catered to in my career and am probably a little bit spoiled. I'm telling you now, Leah, don't take any shit from me or Linc. Make us spoil you. You deserve it."

She was about to answer she'd never been spoiled in her life, but he was pressing his cock into her pussy and all other thoughts disintegrated into dust. She moaned and panted as he pushed in relentlessly, stretching her cunt and rubbing against her G-spot. When he was in all the way, she wrapped her legs around his waist, pulling him down for a long, hot kiss while her pussy adjusted to being so full. He was a big man, and she was crammed full of cock.

Her senses whirled and tumbled. She could feel his hard, muscular body pressing her into the mattress. His musky male scent enveloped her, the rough hair on his body brushing her skin and nipples, sending shivers to her pussy. She was beginning to understand why people were so excited about sex. This was what songs and poems were written about.

He started moving, pulling almost all the way out, before pressing back in. Her toes curled with each stroke, sending shivers of pleasure and arousal through her body and straight to her clit. With each thrust, he rubbed against her clit, and soon she was on the edge again, panting and digging her nails into his back. He bent his head and captured her nipple into his mouth, nibbling and sucking until she was moving under him frantically, trying to get the friction she needed to send her over.

He nipped at the soft skin of her shoulder and then licked at the wound. "Easy, honey. I'll make sure you get what you need." He sped up his thrusts and she cried out from the intensity of feeling. He reached between them and ran his fingers around her already swollen and sensitive clit.

"Justin!"

The pleasure was almost painful. Nothing had ever felt this good or right. He thrust in one final time and froze, his head thrown back, his teeth clenched. She felt him pulse inside her and it spurred her orgasm on until they both collapsed on the bed, sweaty, sated, and exhausted.

They both lay there for a while until he pulled away slowly. "I need to take care of the condom, honey. I'll be right back."

She felt cold as he left the bed, but he wasn't gone long. He quickly cleaned her thighs with a warm washcloth before sliding into bed next to her. She felt happy, cared for, and comfortable. Making love with Justin was something she could never have imagined. It was better than anything she'd read in a book.

She didn't want to move but was unsure as to the protocol now. Was she supposed to get up, get dressed, and head home? She stroked his bicep and pressed a kiss to his chest.

"I guess it's getting pretty late."

"Mmmm, I guess so." Justin's voice rumbled in his chest. He sounded half asleep.

She wriggled in his arms until she found the perfect spot to sleep, her head pillowed on his shoulder. "I have to work tomorrow. I'm usually not up this late."

She didn't really know how late it was, but she couldn't come right out and ask him if he wanted her to leave.

"Do you need me to set an alarm for the morning? I'm not a morning person, so I don't usually get up early."

She relaxed. He wanted her to stay. "I'm an early bird. I wake up at the same time every morning. No need to set an alarm."

She felt rather than heard his chuckle. "How efficient. Close your beautiful brown eyes, and get some sleep, honey. I'm going to want to make love again in the morning. Fuck, I may wake you up in the middle of the night."

She pressed closer and let sleep overtake her, loving the feel of Justin's body next to hers and wondering how long she would have him in her life.

* * * *

The house was finally quiet. Linc stretched out his legs in front of the fireplace and drank a long swallow of whiskey. He'd lost track of the time he'd been sitting here, hearing the sounds of Justin making love to Leah.

At one point, she'd screamed Justin's name and Linc's heart had twisted in his chest. He'd known it would be painful to step aside, to give Leah up, but he wasn't prepared for how excruciating it would be. It was like being cut open and laid bare with no anesthesia. Even the half bottle of whiskey hadn't been able to deaden the pain inside him.

He wanted to be with her.

Linc knew he'd hurt her earlier. He hadn't wanted to, and it hurt him even more to know he had. Justin had turned her toward him, and Leah had looked at him with her aroused expression and her lips swollen from Justin's kiss. It had taken every ounce of his strength not to pull her into his arms and kiss her the way he'd imagined a thousand times. In those fantasies, there was nothing keeping them apart. No secrets between them.

At one point, he'd weakened and stumbled upstairs to join them, his desire for Leah blotting out all the reasons they couldn't be together. He'd seen her on her knees in front of Justin, looking innocent and sexy at the same time, and he'd felt something break inside of him. He wouldn't, couldn't, do this to her, or to himself. He never wanted to see her look at him with shame or disappointment in her eyes. He'd seen that look before and he couldn't take it from her.

I'm a fucking coward.

He took another gulp of the burning liquid, enjoying the fire trail it left from his throat to his churning gut. Even Justin didn't know the reason he held himself back from her. After all these years, it was amazing he'd managed to keep this one thing a secret from Justin. They knew everything about each other, but this one thing. But then Linc had become a master at covering this up. No one even suspected the truth. Hell, sometimes he even forgot the truth himself.

He tossed back the last bit of whiskey from the glass and poured himself another.

It was going to be a long night.

Chapter Five

She was having the sexiest, most erotic dream. A warm, wet tongue was licking at her pussy and rough fingers were playing with her nipples. She was so relaxed she let her climax roll right through her, moaning words of encouragement to her dream man.

When the last wave subsided, her eyes snapped open, and her body began to flood with embarrassment. It hadn't been a dream at all. Justin was grinning at her from between her legs. She wanted to crawl away and die when she realized what she had said to him.

He pressed a kiss to the sensitive skin of her inner thigh. "Baby has quite a mouth on her. I hope you liked the orgasm, and yes, ma'am, I do intend to fuck you hard. Although I was planning to take my time."

She clapped her hands over her eyes and groaned. She really didn't have a filthy mouth, but in her dreams she was much more wild and wanton than in real life.

Lick me. Lick me until I come, then give me your big cock hard and fast.

He pried her hands apart with a laugh. "Relax, honey. I like a woman who can say what she wants. Saves me from having to figure it out. I'm just a dumb guy, remember?"

She shouldn't feel self-conscious. She was the same woman he had woken in the middle of the night with caressing hands and had fucked her long and slow, taking his time until they both couldn't hold back any longer. His mouth and hands had explored her entire body. There were no secrets there. She wanted this and there was no shame in letting him know.

"I thought I was dreaming."

He reached into the nightstand and snagged another condom. "A dream, huh? If that's how you are in your dreams, you're going to have to tell me all of your dreams. We'll live them out one by one." He flipped her over on her stomach before she had time to even reply. "This morning, however, we're going to live out one of my dreams. On your hands and knees, honey."

She gave him a withering look over her shoulder but pushed to her knees. She wasn't fooling anyone. She wanted him inside her and he knew it. She heard the crinkle of the condom wrapper and then he held her hips steady, the head of his cock nudging the lips of her pussy. She tried to press back on it, but his fingers tightened, holding her in place.

"Do you want this, honey? Tell me you want my cock and I'll give it to you."

She tried to break his hold, but he was firmly in control. "I already did."

He ran the tip through her drenched folds, teasing her clit. "Tell me again. I want you to say it when you're awake."

He continued stroking her slit with his cock, making her increasingly desperate for him. She needed him now. She was starting to understand what it was going to mean when he said he was in charge. He was clearly calling the shots at the moment.

"I want your cock. Fuck me with it." The words came out slightly choked, but Justin didn't seem to care.

He patted her on her bottom and whispered, "Good girl," in her ear. He pulled back and thrust into her all the way to the hilt. She keened at the feeling of his cock so deeply inside of her.

He didn't work up to it, but started pounding her hard as she'd asked him. She braced herself on the bed, pushing back with each thrust. She could swear she felt every ridge of his cock rubbing her sensitive spots even through the condom. His fingers tangled in her long hair, pulling her lips back for a wet kiss.

She was close to the edge, her body teetering on the precipice, waiting to go over. He slapped her ass cheek with his hand and the pain quickly turned to heat and pleasure. She wriggled her ass in provocation and he did it again and again until she screamed her climax. Her body trembled and she went down, her cheek pressed to the bed. She gave herself up to the waves as she felt him thrust one last time and groan his pleasure with her body. She felt his cock pulse inside of her and his fingers loosened their hold on the long strands of her hair.

He pulled out and she stretched out on the bed while he dealt with the condom. He came back to bed and pulled her close.

"Hell of a morning wake-up call. I could get used to this. You just might turn me into a morning person, honey."

She kissed his smiling mouth and felt a moment of fear. She could get used to this, as well.

* * * *

"I'll have the pancake breakfast with maple syrup, two, no, three slices of bacon, and whole-wheat toast. How about an order of those cinnamon apples, too? What are you having, honey?"

Leah gaped at the amount of food Justin was planning to ingest at breakfast. She usually had a muffin and some orange juice. He'd dragged her to the diner this morning after stopping at her home so she could shower and change for work. He insisted on feeding her breakfast after their, as he termed it, night of debauchery. She had to admit she was hungrier than normal. Perhaps he was right that a night of lovemaking had to be fueled with carbs.

"I'll have one of the Belgian waffles with strawberries."

Justin beamed in approval. Somehow, she'd known he wouldn't have been happy about a bran muffin eaten as she walked to the bookstore.

She sipped her coffee. "I rarely eat a real breakfast. I usually just grab a muffin on the way to work."

Justin leaned back in the booth, looking devastatingly handsome for so early in the morning. "Breakfast is the most important meal of the day. When I'm up early enough to eat it, that is."

"You're a night owl, I take it?"

He shrugged and took a large gulp of his cranberry juice. "I am now. After years of touring, performing concerts, traveling, and sleeping during the day, my body clock has adjusted to this vampire-like lifestyle. Opening a nightclub was a no-brainer. We'd already been living the hours for years."

She didn't want to talk about Linc, but couldn't seem to help herself. She'd been thinking about him all morning. Last night had been wonderful, but without Linc, it was as if something was missing. She'd grown up in a ménage house and had always wanted the lifestyle for herself.

"How long have you known Linc? Was he a musician, too?"

Justin grinned. "I was at the University of Washington when I met Linc. He was already managing a couple of bands in the Seattle music scene. Damn, he was one of the smartest guys I'd ever met. I was working for drinks at the bar where he found me. He gave us some advice, dragged us to an audition at another bar, and next thing I know we're making actual cash every night. He negotiated for a piece of the door."

"And then you became a star."

Justin threw back his head and laughed. "I wish it had been that easy, honey. I dropped out of school, pissed off my parents, and went on the road. We spent the next three years playing bars, nightclubs, county fairs, hell, any place we could get booked in. Linc pooled every cent he had and underwrote a demo tape. He sent it to every record company in town. We finally got a contract with Place Records. Everything happened from there. If it weren't for Linc, I probably would still be playing dive bars for drinks. Fuck, I'd have given up by now. Gone into the family business like my dad wanted me to."

The waitress came by and warmed up her coffee. "What's the family business?"

"Furniture. My parents were third-generation furniture builders. Handcrafted tables, chairs, beds. Stuff like that. They had a retail store in Seattle. Still do, actually. My sister runs it now. My parents are retired. I paid off their house after my first album."

"That's sweet. You're close to your family then?"

"I guess so. I see them at all the major holidays. They're coming here for Easter. I went there for Christmas. They still bug me about getting my college degree."

Their plates were set in front of them and Leah's stomach growled. She pressed a hand to her belly and grimaced. "I guess I was hungrier than I thought."

Justin waggled his eyebrows. "We worked up an appetite last night." He signaled to the waitress for coffee, pushing away his empty juice glass.

"What about you? I know you have a cousin who's a deputy. Do you have other family?"

The first bite of her waffle was heaven. She really ought to make time to eat breakfast more often.

"My parents passed away when I was eight. My mother and dads were flying back from Atlanta. One of my dads was flying their small-engine plane. They lost oil pressure over northern Florida and crashed."

Justin grabbed her hand. "Aw, honey, I'm sorry. I wouldn't have asked if I'd known it was so sad."

She shook her head. "It was twenty years ago. I've learned to accept what I can't change. I went to live with my aunt and uncles. I already spent a great deal of time with them. In fact, I was staying with them when my parents were on their trip. Well, me and my brother, Gabe. We grew up as their children. They had a son, Jason, and three daughters who were younger than me.

"My aunt and uncle became my second parents. Gabe and Jason are, well, were, like brothers. The bookstore belonged to one of my dads. My aunt ran it until I was out of college. Then I took it over. My other dad ran an auto repair business. It's all closed up, of course. At one point, I thought Gabe would take it over. It didn't work out that way."

"I don't think I've met Gabe. I have met Deputy Jason."

She wasn't sure what to say about her brother. What used to be so simple wasn't anymore. "You haven't met him because he left town about two years ago. When he came back from Iraq, he had some anger issues. He and Jason were dating a beautiful girl named Samantha. We all thought they would get married. Then Iraq happened, and Jason came back changed, but Gabe...Gabe came back a different person. He and Jason fought and eventually Gabe left."

She looked into Justin's sympathetic blue eyes. "He's coming home in a day or two. He's going to stay with me. He says he's all better now."

"Do you believe him?"

It was an easy question. "Yes, I do. He even sounds different on the phone. Sure of himself. Commanding, but calm. Yes, I think he's better now."

Justin played with her fingers. "Maybe they'll all three get back together."

She shook her head. "No. Samantha left town even before Gabe did. She couldn't take the anger and issues. Jason blamed Gabe, and Gabe blamed himself. It's sad really. Gabe and Jason always wanted to share a woman like my parents and Jason's parents did."

"Linc and I feel the same way. There's something bonding about loving the same woman. Making her happy, bringing her pleasure. It's more than I've ever felt on my own."

She pushed her plate away, her appetite gone. "Then being with me is stupid. Linc doesn't want me. If you want to share a woman, you need to find someone else."

Justin lifted her hand and kissed her knuckles. "Bossy, aren't you? We're not in the bedroom, so I guess it's okay." He pinned her to her seat with his stare. "Listen to me, honey. Linc wants you. He's wearing his ass as a hat right now, but he wants you. Just be patient."

"He said—"

Justin held up his hand. "I don't care what he said. Men say shit. Growing up with two males, I would imagine you know by now men say things they often don't mean and later regret. Linc wants you. I know he's hurt you so I wouldn't blame you if you made him grovel when he finally does come to his senses. I wouldn't mind watching him beg."

A picture of Linc on his knees, begging and contrite, made her smile. "He'd have to beg and grovel an awful lot. If he really wants me, that means he was a royal jerk last night."

Justin sighed. "He was. I thought for sure he would join us. He has a higher sex drive than I do, and I know you turn him on, honey."

Leah gulped her coffee. "Higher than yours? Holy crap, maybe it's just as well I'm only with you. There's no way I could keep both of you happy."

Justin tucked into the cinnamon apples with gusto. "You'll do fine. We're not unreasonable men. We can control ourselves. Although, it's not easy around you."

"You made it look easy these last months. In fact, Linc made it look damn easy at the Halloween party. Those two blondes looked ready and willing to help with any libido problem either of you might have."

She pressed her lips together. She sounded jealous, which she was. She also sounded like a shrew. It wasn't attractive and right now she wasn't feeling too great about herself.

Justin pushed her plate back in front of her, his jaw tight. She'd managed to piss him off and it was only nine in the morning.

"First of all, finish your breakfast. Second, I wasn't with those two blondes. Third, Linc's being a jackass."

She slumped in the booth. "I'm sorry. I hate being jealous. I fucking hate being insecure. This isn't fun for me. I don't like myself at the moment."

He nodded. "Then stop. You don't have any reason to be jealous or insecure. We only want you. I told you earlier. Make Linc and I toe the line, behave ourselves, spoil you. Be confident. If anyone walks away from this relationship, it will be you. You hold all the cards." He picked up her fork and held it out. "Normally, I don't hand over the power in a relationship like I just did. But, lady, if anyone needed the power it's you. You've got us on our knees, Leah. It's up to you how you're going to treat us now that we're there."

She took the fork he was offering and resumed eating her waffles. She'd never held all the power in a relationship, but Justin was right. If this was going to work out, she needed to woman up right now. No more feeling insecure and inadequate. These men were going to behave and treat her the way she deserved to be treated.

Now, what was she going to do about Linc?

* * * *

She couldn't seem to stop yawning. She was reading a book about a dog that ran away from home to a group of toddlers and their mothers, and it wasn't the most riveting stuff. After every other page, she would duck behind the book and yawn again. Justin had kept her up most of the night. Not that she was complaining. She'd pick hot sex with the sexiest man alive over sleep any day.

"And Scooter was happy to be home with his humans. The end."

The kids started getting restless now that the story was over. She pointed to the front table and froze. Gabe was standing there nibbling on a cookie, a small smile on his face. She cleared her throat, the emotion she felt thick. She hadn't seen him in two years, and the last she had, he'd been angry and bitter. Today, he looked calm and in control.

"There's cookies and juice at the front table. Any children's book purchased today will be fifteen percent off. Thanks for coming to Story Time with Leah. Next week, we'll be reading a story about a ferret who saves his family."

He stood there patiently, not saying a word, while she waited on all the customers. Finally, the last one left the store and it was only the two of them. She walked up to the door, locked it, and flipped the sign to Closed. She couldn't help herself any longer. She launched herself at him, hugging him and crying. She hadn't realized how much she'd missed him until this moment. She also hadn't expressed her anger. She started beating on his chest with her hands.

"Damn you, Gabe. Damn you. Why did you have to stay away so long? Damn you! I'm so angry with you. I'm so pissed, you selfish son of a bitch!"

He let her beat on him until she was exhausted, helping her into a chair when she was done. He sat across from her, holding her hand.

"Good for you, sis." His voice was soft, but firm.

She tried smacking his hand away, but he held on tight. "Good for me?"

"Yes, good for you. I deserve every bit of your anger. I was a selfish son of a bitch and I'm sorry." He squeezed her fingers. "I'm sorry I had to leave you. I'm sorry I stayed away so long. You know, the Leah I used to know wouldn't have given me hell. I like this girl."

Her lips twisted. The anger was already draining away. She hadn't expected a sincere apology within five minutes of his return. He had never been one for acknowledging his mistakes in the past. In fact, she would have called him downright pigheaded and stubborn as a mule.

Her newfound resolve was firm. She'd turned a corner this morning in bed with Justin. She wasn't powerless. Acting insecure and weak was getting old and it wasn't any fun. "I'm trying something new. I've decided to make sure the men in my life treat me well. You didn't."

He nodded. "I know. It's something I intend to rectify now that I'm home." He grabbed another cookie. "Damn, I missed your cookies. Chocolate chip was always my favorite, though."

"You and Jason both."

A flicker of sadness crossed his features. "How pissed off is Jason?"

"Angry. Confused. Frustrated. Same as me. Although he'll probably punch you."

Gabe smiled. "I'll give him one free one. He deserves it." He looked her over. "You look good, sis. Happy. The store seems to be doing well, too."

"I have the same issues all brick-and-mortar bookstores have, but luckily the town has been very loyal."

Gabe stood up and looked out the large front window that looked over the street. "That's Plenty for you. Loyal. I can't believe how much the town has changed in just two years. New businesses. New faces. Hell, I drove by some sort of nightclub on the outskirts of town on my way here. I think the name was Party Like A Rock Star. We actually have a nightclub in this town. Never thought I'd see the day."

"That club belongs to Justin Reynolds and his manager, Linc Davis. They came here to retire."

Gabe's eyebrows went up. "The Justin Reynolds? I've got some of his music on my phone."

She licked her lips and gathered up all her courage. "I'm dating him."

Gabe laughed and shook his head. "I have been gone a long time. My bookworm sister is dating a rock star."

"I don't really think of him that way. He's really a nice man. We have a lot in common. Books, movies, television."

She tried to stop her yawn, but didn't succeed. She could use a nap, but she wasn't going to get one. Gabe looked at her through narrowed eyes.

"You look tired, sis. Has said rock star been keeping you up? Do I need to have a talk with him about his intentions?"

She stood up and poked him in the chest. "Don't you dare, Gabriel Christopher Holt. You can't come waltzing in here and start acting the big brother."

"I'll always be your big brother. Tell me one thing. Is this guy treating you right?"

She thought about how Linc had hurt her not once, but twice now. He certainly wasn't treating her right, and she'd been thinking about it all day and how she was going to handle it. Around lunchtime she'd made the decision he was going to have to come to her with a damn good explanation and some heavy-duty groveling and begging. She wasn't going to be the girl who faded into the background anymore. If he truly wanted her as Justin said he did, he was going to have to show her in every way.

"Justin treats me great. No complaints there."

It wasn't the complete truth, but she didn't need Gabe pounding down Linc's door. She pulled her spare house key out of the drawer by the cash register and handed it to her brother.

"I need to open the store back up. You can make yourself at home in the spare room. Tonight we're having dinner with Jason at Charlie's."

Gabe started to protest but she waved him off. "No excuses. Leah has spoken. You can start dealing with the anger now. It won't get any better if you wait a day or two. If anything, he'll be hurt that you didn't see him right away. Besides, I know you love Charlie's pizza."

Gabe chuckled as he headed out the door. "I do love this new woman, sis. I'll just say 'Yes, ma'am,' and head home. If that's okay with you?"

He tried to look humble but he couldn't pull it off. This new Gabe was far too confident and self-assured. Whatever had happened to him in the last two years had been profound.

"It's okay with me." Gabe started to leave, but she caught his arm. "I like the new you, by the way. I really like this guy."

He kissed her forehead. "Thanks, sis. I like this guy, too. Let's hope everyone in Plenty likes him. I have a bad reputation to live down."

Gabe headed out of the store. It was the way in small towns. People got put in boxes, and others liked to keep them there. Both she and Gabe were going to have to work long and hard to claw their way out of that trap. It looked like they were both well on their way.

Chapter Six

It had been the worst week of Linc's life. That was saying something. Worse than when his mother had remarried and his stepfather was a jerk. Worse than just about every single day at school. Worse than when his grandmother died on his tenth birthday. Every single day had been a slow torture. There wasn't enough whiskey to deaden the pain.

He'd spent the time trying to avoid Leah, and to his chagrin it was working, most of the time. She apparently didn't want to see him any more than he wanted to see her. Not seeing her hadn't helped, however. Although he didn't see her in their home, he knew she had been there. Her scent was everywhere, imprinted on the sofa, the bathroom, even the kitchen. It was driving him slowly insane. Several times he had almost given in and sought her out, begged for forgiveness. Only the memory of his family's disappointed faces held him back. He never wanted to see that again.

He leaned his forehead against the glass of the window overlooking the nightclub, a crush of bodies on the dance floor below. It had been his idea to build their office on the second floor with a view to the floor below. He could keep an eye on everything going on but stay out of the spotlight. People wondered if he was jealous of Justin's fame, but Linc had never sought attention. It suited him fine to be a player behind the scenes, making the power deals. He'd found something he excelled at. He knew, without conceit, he was one of the best. He'd worked hard to make sure of it.

"Hiding in here?" Justin was wearing a smirk. He tossed his keys on his desk and joined Linc at the window.

"No, I'm not. I was signing invoices. Where the hell have you been? The crew started changing the stage, and when I asked why, Cheryl said it was on your orders. What's going on?"

Justin waggled his eyebrows. "I had an early dinner with Leah, then we went back to our house for some…one-on-one time. Too bad you weren't there. But I guess you're not attracted to her, so it's no big deal, huh?"

Linc ground his teeth together. He was getting tired of Justin's not-so-subtle digs. "Back off. I'd hate to mess up your pretty-boy face."

"Go for it. It'd be the first emotion you've shown in over a week. As for the stage, I did tell Cheryl to change it. Brayden, Falk, and Josh are going to play a set tonight. Ava is their new lead singer. I heard them when Leah and I went for dinner on Sunday and they sound great. It's classic-rock night, so I asked them to play. Any issues with it?"

Linc had wondered where Justin disappeared to on Sunday. They were already socializing like a *couple*. His gut twisted but he pushed the feeling away. He didn't have the luxury.

"None. I need—" A rap on the door interrupted him. It was probably Cheryl. She loved the nights when both he and Justin were in attendance. If any sticky situation came up, she could handle it fine on her own, but she liked them to be aware of what was happening at all times. She was a damn fine general manager and they were lucky to have her.

Justin pulled the door open and a smiling Bobbi stood on the other side, looking New York chic. She'd always had a distinctive style about her whether it was clothes, cars, or even food. Justin hugged her with a grin.

"Hey, girl. You're far away from New York. What brings you to our stomping grounds?"

Linc hugged her, too, but was instantly on guard. He liked Bobbi. She was a good promoter and a friendly woman. She wasn't this friendly, however. She wasn't what Linc would call a friend. She was an acquaintance. An acquaintance who had traveled a couple of thousand miles from the city that never slept.

She wanted something.

Linc had a pretty good idea what the something was. Bobbi didn't take being turned down well.

"I came to see your nightclub. I was in South Beach for some business and decided to detour here. You weren't kidding about it being a small town. There's isn't even a hotel. I had to book a room in Orlando."

Justin helped Bobbi with her coat, hanging it on the coat tree in the corner. "Most people rent cabins on the outskirts of town. I'm told there used to be a bed-and-breakfast, but the woman who runs it got too old and she closed it. Can I get you a drink?"

Bobbi perched on one of the overstuffed leather chairs and crossed her legs, showing off her clearly designer footwear. Leah liked to wear sneakers or practical, low-heeled shoes. Linc wasn't sure how Bobbi walked on those skyscraper heels. He much preferred a woman who wasn't too obvious.

"I'd love a martini, Justin. And before you ask, I'm not driving. I have a limo and driver tonight. I don't know these roads so it seemed the logical thing to do."

Justin laughed. "Most people use GPS, Bobbi, but then you're not most people." He hit the intercom and ordered the drink. "It will be right up. What were you doing in South Beach?"

"It was business mostly. Scouting a new band with a friend. He asked my opinion. Also, a few days in warmer weather. New York is colder than hell this time of year. A girl can only take so much. I'm looking forward to a week in St. Maarten next month."

Linc perched on the edge of the desk. "Was the band worth the trip?"

She sighed and pursed her lips. "No. Music these days is in a dismal state. Which is why I'm here actually."

A discreet waitress brought Bobbi's drink and she sipped at it before making a face and setting it on the table next to her. "I know you said you weren't interested in a concert tour. But I came here to talk to you personally. The music business is in disarray and it needs a big star over the age of eighteen. It needs you, Justin."

Justin sat in the chair opposite hers and shook his head. "I'm flattered, Bobbi, but I'm retired. I like being retired. I might record some music now and then, but I don't want to tour anymore. I'm too old for that shit."

Bobbi wasn't going to give up. She leaned forward, her manner urgent. "You need this tour. Do you want people to forget who you are? Forget all the music? You'll become a has-been if you aren't careful. How can you even keep yourself in the news if you live out here in Bumble Fuck? Did you fire your publicist? Foolish move, Justin."

Justin caught his eye, but Linc only shrugged. It was Justin's call. If he wanted to do the tour, Linc would support him. If he didn't want to, Linc was more than happy. Justin was right. They were too damn old to be touring and the business wasn't fun anymore.

"I did fire my publicist. I moved here to become a has-been. I don't need this tour. I don't want my name in the papers. I just want to live a quiet, ordinary life. And the town's name is Plenty. Not Bumble Fuck, if you please. Have a little respect for the choices I've made. If people forget my music, then it must not have been memorable."

Justin stood as if the discussion was over. Bobbi looked angry but she composed her features. By the time she spoke again, she looked completely serene.

"Your music is memorable. I'm not giving up. I'm going to keep trying to convince you if you don't mind and see if I can change your mind."

Justin shook his head. "You're welcome to try, but I won't change my mind."

Bobbi stood and headed for the door. "Maybe I'll see what's so great about this town. Why you won't leave it even for a short time." She twisted the doorknob, but paused. "This tour could be a triumph for you. I'll make you the headliner. I'll pay you twice the standard rate. Think about that. The kind of financial security others can only dream about. The kind of money you could pass down to those children you're always talking about having. You'd move from rich to super rich."

The click of her heels on the stairs was the only sound in the room. Linc watched through the window as she crossed the crowded nightclub and headed out the door. He turned back to his best friend.

"Well, that was interesting. I never thought she'd show up here to try and convince you. I sure didn't see that coming. Did you?"

Justin laughed. "Fuck no. Bobbi outside of a major metropolitan city? Not in a million years." He headed for the door. "I'm going to walk around, see how things are going. Are you coming?"

Linc sat behind the large oak desk. He had a phone call to make. Something wasn't adding up. "I'll be down in a few minutes. I still have some work to do."

As soon as the door closed, he picked up the phone and dialed a couple of guys he hadn't talked to in a long time.

"Logan, it's Linc Davis. How are you?"

The man on the other end laughed. "Linc, man, how the hell are you? I haven't talked to you in forever."

Linc propped his legs on his desk. "I'm doing okay. Listen, I need to hire you and Meyer. I need you to check out somebody for me."

"You got it. Who is it?"

"Bobbi Blackwell. Bobbi with an 'i.' She's a concert promoter."

"The full dossier? Personal, business, and financial?"

"Yes. How soon can you get it?"

He heard Logan talking to someone and then he was back. "Give me about a couple of weeks, hopefully less. Meyer is already working it, but the personal stuff could take some time."

Linc hung up and smiled, leaning back in the chair. He was a suspicious, careful man, and Bobbi's behavior was setting off warning bells in his brain. He needed to see what the sophisticated Ms. Blackwell was up to. He was certain it wasn't anything good.

* * * *

The band was actually quite good. Ava had a deep, husky voice and it was currently blending with Falk's to belt out a cover of "Money for Nothing." Brayden was on drums and Falk and Josh were playing guitar. Or bass. Or something like that. Leah didn't know a great deal about musical instruments, but she knew good music when she heard it. The four of them were great.

"Miss me?" Justin was behind her, his hand on her shoulder, his low, warm voice in her ear.

She turned and kissed him, not caring if anyone watched. After their breakfast at the diner last week, the secret was out. Everyone in town was talking about how smitten the rock star was with their little hometown bookworm. She'd had several women stop her tonight and ask her advice about men. She'd almost laughed hysterically. What she knew about men would fit on the head of a pin. Apparently, the town thought she had some kind of wisdom regarding catching an elusive male. If they only knew.

The truth was that as wonderful as the last week with Justin had been, her heart still ached with missing Linc. It felt incomplete. Wrong, somehow. Justin was right. It was more when it was all three of them.

Or it would be more if Linc wasn't avoiding her. It wasn't easy to avoid someone in a town the size of Plenty, but somehow Linc had managed it. She wanted to find him and kick him in the shins, but it wouldn't make any difference. Justin assured her Linc would come around in his own time. She simply needed to be patient.

Justin had learned a lesson about Leah the day he told her that.

She was an impatient person, constantly pushing things forward. It made her a good businesswoman, but a frustrated human being. Justin had simply laughed and told her he was relieved she had some imperfections. Otherwise, she was intimidating. Then he'd taken her to bed and showed her how much he liked all her imperfections.

"I did miss you. Is everything okay?" she asked.

He sat next to her and put his arm around her shoulders, pulling her close. She let his sexy scent envelop her and leaned closer to his strong frame. She always felt so petite and protected when he was around.

"It's fine, just making sure things are running smoothly. We had a visitor earlier. I'll tell you about it later."

She nodded and picked up her glass, draining the last drops of juice. She didn't like to drink much when she had to work the next day. She grabbed her purse and tugged on Justin's sleeve.

"I'm heading to the ladies' room. I'll be right back."

He smiled and nodded and helped her out of her chair. She hummed with the music all the way to the back of the nightclub. She was turning the corner to the restrooms when a large body slammed into hers. She almost went down but was able to grab the wall to hold herself up, but dropped her handbag.

"Earl! For heaven's sake, you almost sent me to the floor." She chuckled and bent to pick up her purse. She'd known Earl since kindergarten. He was married with a couple of kids now, but she'd heard he and Tina were having troubles. She wasn't completely surprised. Earl always had been a hell-raiser when they were younger.

She was shocked when his large male hand grabbed her ass and his other pulled her close. His breath stank of whiskey and cigarettes and she started to struggle.

"Let me go! Earl, let me go this minute!"

She kicked as hard as she could, but in his inebriated state he seemed immune to the pain. She hoped he'd have giant bruises tomorrow.

"Relax, Leah. I just want some of what you're handing out to rock royalty. What's the matter? Country boys ain't good enough for you? A man needs to have a Ferrari or something?"

She pushed against his chest. "He doesn't have a Ferrari, you jerk. Let me go."

A hand came out of nowhere and clapped down on Earl's arm.

"Get your hands off my woman. I fucking mean it, asshole. Let her go, or I will personally rip your leg from its socket and beat the ever-loving shit out of you with it."

Linc.

* * * *

Linc twisted the man's arm behind his back. He fought to stay in control of his rage. When he'd seen that man grab Leah, he'd seen red. She'd looked so frightened and the man was twice her size. No one was going to hurt Leah. Ever.

"Hey, hey, man, she came on to me. She grabbed me."

Linc twisted the arm a little harder and the man howled in outrage. He wasn't going to break the appendage, although he was sorely tempted, but he wanted to make sure this guy got the message loud and clear. He leaned down and looked into the drunk's eyes.

"Listen to me, and listen closely. Leah Holt is under my protection. I saw you grab her and we don't allow the harassment of our female patrons here. Do you understand?"

The man nodded slowly. He seemed to be sobering up. "I want you out of this bar. Now. You are to never come back. You are to never speak to Leah again. I don't even want you thinking about Leah. Do you understand?"

The man swallowed hard and nodded again just as two of his bouncers showed up.

"Boss, can we help here?"

Linc let the arm go and stepped back. "Escort this gentleman to his vehicle. Stay there until he is off the property. Also, post his picture at the door. He's banned from the club."

The bouncers took the man away and Linc turned back to Leah to make sure she was okay and unhurt. If he'd expected gratitude he was going to be disappointed. She was scowling, her toe tapping against the wood floor. Her arms were crossed across her chest.

Damn, she's cute and sexy when she's mad.

"I suppose you're proud of yourself, acting like a badass with Earl. He was drunk and didn't know what he was doing."

Linc stepped closer and her clean, floral scent swamped his senses. He felt his entire body respond, including his cock, pressing against the fly of his jeans. He willed it to behave, thinking serene thoughts.

"He was drunk, but I think he knew exactly what he was doing. He wasn't that impaired. Should I have let him paw you?"

She stood ramrod straight and poked him in the chest with her finger. "I had it under control."

He laughed. "That was under control? No, baby, you did not have him under control. You're lucky I showed up."

She stomped her foot. "Don't call me 'baby.' I'm not your woman, either. You're not attracted to me, remember?"

Her voice shook, but she stood her ground. He felt his heart plummet.

"Did Justin tell you that?"

She snorted. "No. I heard it from your own lips. That day in the bookstore when Justin asked me out. You made it clear. I'm not your type. Well, news flash, you arrogant asshole, you're not my type either. Any man who wants to be with me is going to have to treat me like I'm important to him. He needs to put me first. Personally, I don't think you're capable of it."

He wanted to pull her into his arms and show her just how important to him she was. He wanted to say he was sorry and make everything better. He wanted to swear he would put her first. He opened his mouth but didn't know what to say. It was all such a mess.

"Cat got your tongue?"

Words only seemed to get him in trouble. He took her arm, her skin soft under his fingers, and guided her to where Justin sat. She didn't say anything else, simply glared at him with those dark-brown eyes.

"You need to take care of your woman. I'll be in the office."

He turned and stomped up the stairs before Justin could question him. He needed some private time to deal with this. Something had to give, and he feared it might be him. The last thing he wanted was for Leah to think badly of herself because he wasn't with her. She wasn't lacking anything. It was him.

He might have to tell her the truth.

Chapter Seven

Leah punched her pillow and tried to get comfortable. Seeing Linc tonight had thrown off her equilibrium. He was a jerk, but her body couldn't help responding to him. Feeling his body close to hers, smelling his sexy scent, she'd wanted to throw herself into his arms.

After she stomped on his foot, of course.

The thing was she didn't really think Linc was a jerk. He hadn't acted like a jerk. He'd been nothing but nice to her. He wasn't attracted to her, that was all. It didn't make him a jerk.

She threw her pillow down and decided to head into the kitchen for some herbal tea to relax her. She certainly wasn't going to sleep in the mood she was in at the moment.

A tap on her window made her freeze in place. She waited, only to hear the tap again. She walked cautiously to the window and peeked through the curtain, almost fainting when she saw a face.

She pressed a hand to her galloping heart and took a deep breath before pushing the curtains aside and pulling up the sash.

"Lincoln Davis, you almost gave me a heart attack. How long have you been standing there?"

He looked handsome, even in the dim light from the street, his dark hair shiny and his shoulders wide.

"I just got here. Geez, baby, do you think I'm some sort of Peeping Tom?"

She hardened her already softening heart. "How would I know? And I told you not to call me 'baby.' I'm not your baby. What are you doing here in the middle of the night anyway?"

"Trying to scare unsuspecting homeowners, apparently." His

voice was hushed but amused. "I didn't want to ring the doorbell and wake up your brother. I heard he was back in town."

"Gabe is in Orlando visiting an old friend."

She heard the sound of crickets in the background.

"Can I come in?" he asked.

"Why?"

"I need to talk to you. I need to tell you something. Things aren't what they seem."

"I don't think we have anything to talk about."

"Please, Leah. I have to talk to you. When I'm done, I'll go. I promise. Please."

If he hadn't said "please" twice she would have slammed the window and pulled the curtains. But his voice had softened into a plea and she still felt so much for him. She was such a wimp.

"You have ten minutes. Not a second more. Come to the front door."

* * * *

How could he possibly say everything he needed to say in ten minutes? He'd been hiding the truth pretty much his entire life and now he had to bare his soul in under ten minutes.

He entered her home and pulled off his jacket. It had been fucking cold out there and her home was warm and welcoming. If only he could say that about Leah. She had her lips pressed together and her arms crossed protectively over her chest as if she was bracing herself for more hurt. He didn't want to hurt her anymore. That was why he was here.

"I don't suppose I could have some coffee. It's cold out there."

She lifted her chin. "You won't be here long enough to have coffee. So, what did you want to talk about?"

Linc sat down on the overstuffed sofa, her living room comfortable and inviting, the decor tasteful and not overdone. Just like Leah herself.

"I don't really know how to tell you this. I've never told anyone else what I'm about to tell you. The only people who know are my parents and brother and sister."

"Then why are you telling me now?"

"Because I care too much about you to hurt you anymore. I'm so sorry you were hurt in the first place. You're the last person I'd ever want to hurt. I don't want you to think the reason I've pulled away is you. It doesn't have a damn thing to do with you. It's all me. I'm not good enough for you."

He had her attention. She sat down in the adjacent armchair. "The old, 'it's not you, it's me' routine? My aunt always said if a man tells you he's not good enough for you, believe it. He knows himself better than you do."

Linc laughed, despite the circumstances. "Your aunt sounds like a wise woman. I'd like to meet her sometime."

"You're running out of time, Linc."

He sighed. "When I met you, I was instantly attracted to you. You're a beautiful woman."

Her expression grew stormy and she jumped up from the chair and walked to the window, staring out into the darkness. "Liar. I heard you tell Justin you weren't attracted to me. Don't lie now to spare my feelings."

He stood up and crossed the room, turning her so he was looking into her brown eyes. They were bright with unshed tears and Linc knew he was the asshole who had put them there. He needed to put things right.

"You're a beautiful woman, Leah. Inside and out. You're funny, and soft-hearted, and damn it all, you're probably the smartest woman I've ever met."

She frowned. "You make it sound like a bad thing."

He stepped back. He needed to put some space between the two of them or he was going to pull her into his arms and kiss her pink lips.

He'd fantasized about it a million times but had never been this close to doing it before.

"It isn't a bad thing, of course." He turned and started pacing. "I never went to college. My grades weren't good enough to get in. I barely scraped by in school."

"Oh. Not going to college is nothing to be ashamed of, Linc. My degree is in history. That makes me qualified to ask someone if they want fries with their hamburger."

It was hard to look at her sweet face. He didn't want to see her expression of horror when he told her.

"It's more than not having a college degree. Much more. You're intelligent. You should have an intelligent man at your side. Not someone like me. Someone who's stupid."

She shook her head. "Justin says you're the smartest man he knows. You made him a star and, according to him, a yacht-load of money. How can you call yourself stupid? That's insane."

"It was insane falling for a woman who loves books. You love books."

She threw up her hands in frustration. "Yes, I love books. Is that a crime? I've always loved to read. Don't you? You come to the bookstore every week."

He closed his eyes and gathered every ounce of courage he had inside. "I come to the bookstore every week to see you. I don't read the books I buy there."

She blinked. "You don't like to read. That's okay. You don't have to love books. It's not a requirement."

"It's not that I don't like to read." His fingers tightened on the mantel until the knuckles were white. He'd heard somewhere that the truth would set him free.

"I can't read. I'm illiterate."

* * * *

"That's impossible. Everyone can read."

Even as she said it, she knew it wasn't true. As someone who volunteered to help children learn to read, she knew that literacy was an issue in America. In the orientation class she attended, they had said one in seven adults read below a sixth grade level. It hadn't really made an impact until this moment.

"I mean, of course not everyone can read, but you're a successful businessman. Smart, and respected in your field. You couldn't have done that if you couldn't read."

Linc's expression was tortured, his handsome face gray. She reached out and pressed her hand over his. He was gripping the mantel as if his life depended on it. She pried his fingers off and wrapped her hands around his cold one.

"Obviously I'm not very smart, but I am cunning, Leah. A lifetime of this will make you figure out a million ways to keep people from finding out something like this. God knows, I never wanted you to find out."

"But you showed up here tonight and told me."

He shook his head, his shoulders slumped in defeat. Her heart ached seeing him this way.

"I couldn't let you think there was anything wrong with you. You're perfect. I'm the one who has something wrong with him. I'm the one who's deficient."

She stood there for a long moment, taking a deep breath, and feeling a wave of anger build. She stepped into his personal space and got into his face.

"I'm sorry this has tortured you your entire life. I'm sorry you felt you couldn't trust people with the truth. Carrying something like this around must have been scary and exhausting. But I take exception to how you describe me, Linc. Perfect? How can you think I'm perfect? You must think I'm an incredibly shallow human being. You've dated too many airheads."

He looked shocked. "You couldn't be shallow if you tried. You're amazing."

"But not amazing enough, huh? You thought I'd judge you? Think less of you?"

Her anger was simmering now and she was only getting warmed up. They could have been together and avoided this whole mess if he'd only believed in her.

"I think less of me, why shouldn't you? Fuck, even my parents were disappointed in me. I'll never forget their faces when I would bring home my report cards or when they had teacher conferences. I never wanted to see that look on your face."

Now she was really pissed off. "So this wasn't about sparing me, this was about sparing you? You hurt me, not once, but twice, because you're too chickenshit to see a sad look on my face?"

He hung his head, his eyes sad. "Yes. I didn't want you to see me as less of a man."

She started pacing back and forth, mumbling to herself. Finally, she whirled around and started pointing at him. She knew her face was red with anger, could feel the heat under her skin.

"First, I don't see you as less of a man. I have no idea how you've managed to become so successful with this issue, but it's nothing short of miraculous. You should be very proud of yourself."

She knew she was shouting but wasn't in the mood to stop. He started to speak but she wasn't finished yet.

"Second, I'm not perfect. Not even close. I'm quiet and shy until I get mad. Then, I have a temper. A bad one. You're seeing some of it now, although I'm trying to control it because *I don't want you to think any less of me*."

Her voice was dripping with sarcasm and she didn't care.

"Third, I can see I'm going to have to take control of this situation. You cannot be trusted with this any longer. You'll have to earn back control."

She paced again, shooting him dirty looks. "I'm in charge now and what I say goes." She stopped in front of him and poked him in the chest. "From now on, no more sexy blondes hanging off your arm. I saw those two bimbos on Halloween, you know."

He had the grace to look ashamed. "I can explain about them. I didn't sleep with them, baby. I swear."

"Well, they wanted you to. No more. No more blondes, brunettes, redheads, or anything else. From now on, I'm the only woman in your life. Got that? You're going to toe the line, buddy. You and Justin, both. If some woman comes on to you, you tell her you're spoken for."

"Fourth."

He was smiling now. He didn't look like a man who was being punished or unhappy about anything she was saying.

"Fourth, baby? I can't wait to hear what else I'm going to be doing. So far, I like you taking control."

She swallowed hard. "Shit. Fourth…fourth…" She felt lost for a moment. She needed to hear him say it. "Fourth, is there anything you want to say? There's a few things I'd like to hear."

He pulled her into his arms, so solid and warm. "I have a few things to say. I was lying to Justin when I said I wasn't attracted to you. You're beautiful inside and out. Sexy as hell, too. You've been doing some naughty things in my fantasies, baby."

She blushed, thinking of the fantasies she'd had about him. They'd have to compare notes at a later time.

"And most of all, I'm sorry." His face was close to hers now, his lips mere inches away. "I'm sorry you got hurt because I was a coward. I'm sorry I didn't believe in you enough to tell you. I'm just fucking sorry. You're the first person I've ever told."

She caressed his jaw. "Justin knows, of course."

He shook his head. "No, I've never told Justin."

Shock rippled through her body, the anger starting to drain away.

"How could Justin not know? Linc, how have you kept this a secret for so long?"

He tugged her over to the sofa and pulled her down on his lap. She struggled for a second, but his arms simply tightened around her. She sat still, snuggling close. She really didn't want to move anyway.

"As I said, I'm cunning. I've found a myriad of ways to cover up my reading problem. When we go to a restaurant, I order whatever the special is or I order what someone else orders. I made sure I always ordered last. If I'm alone, I'll ask the waiter for a recommendation."

His hand stroked her back and she felt tingles shoot through her entire body. She'd only dreamed of being this close to him.

"If someone hands me something to read, I'll act busy and ask them if I can get back to them or if they can just summarize it for me. If I can get back to them, I have one of my assistants read it for me. I do all my business verbally, eschewing e-mail or texts. People simply think it's eccentric. If they want to send me an e-mail, they send it to my attorney, accountant, or an assistant. I made sure always to have an attorney look over contracts. Even if I could read, that was just common sense. In the early days, before Justin became famous, we often did business on a handshake."

She was amazed. "But surely Justin must have noticed something?"

He laid his head back on the sofa cushion. "You would think, wouldn't you? I've found that people *see* what they want to *believe*. If he ever noticed anything, his first thought wouldn't be that I couldn't read. His first thought would be that I was being a stubborn asshole, and difficult to do business with. By the time I met Justin, I was twenty-one and had been hiding this for years. I was already practiced at it, and have become even more so as the years have passed."

Her decision was made in an instant. "I won't tell him. You trusted me with this and I won't betray that trust."

He smiled. "I believe you. But telling you has changed things. You didn't judge me. God knows, my own family did. Justin's a good man. He won't judge me. I'm going to tell him the truth. I don't want to ask you to keep secrets from him. It's not a healthy way to start a relationship. Although, I will keep your secret about your temper.

Man, you can really blow your stack. Your face turned three shades of purple. I'll let him find out for himself."

She looked at him through her lashes, her heart beating madly. "Are we in a relationship?"

"It's up to you, Leah. Can you forgive me and give me a chance to show you how I feel? I'll spend as long as it takes making things up to you."

She pretended to pout. "It might take a long time. You were mean."

He quirked an eyebrow. "Mean, huh? I can be mean, baby. You can, too. Fuck, I thought you were going to kick me in the balls a few minutes ago."

She giggled. "I was tempted."

He pushed her back on the couch so he was looming over her, his body pressed close. "You need to know if you kick me, I'll be forced to turn you over my knee. And I'll enjoy every second of it."

She was breathless at the thought. "Justin said the same thing. Are both of you bossy and opinionated?"

Lin chuckled and started nuzzling her ear, making her nipples tighten and her pussy start to drip honey. He smelled delicious and she was dying for him to kiss her.

"Absolutely. Justin and I like to be in charge."

She pressed her hands against his chest to push him away, but instead they started to explore the muscles under her palms. "But I'm in charge. I said so."

He nibbled at her earlobe, making her squirm against him. She could feel the hard ridge of his cock and she had to stop herself from reaching down to cup it with her greedy fingers.

"I'll tell you what, baby. When we're all three together, we'll take a vote. Either you're in charge, or Justin and I are in charge."

"I'll never win. You'll always outvote me. On everything." She was panting as his tongue traced lazy circles on the exposed skin of her shoulders and neck.

"You've got us wrapped around your finger, Leah. I don't think you'll have any complaints. Our goal is to make you the happiest woman in Plenty."

Whoa. That is damn ambitious.

She lifted her head and nipped at his bottom lip. "Then you best get to work. I've been making love to Justin every night for the last week until tonight. You've got a lot of catching up to do."

He grinned, the first real genuine smile of delight she'd ever seen from him. He was so beautiful he took her breath away. He levered himself off the couch, and before she knew what was happening, he'd tossed her over his shoulder in a fireman lift and was heading toward her bedroom.

She squealed when he smacked her bottom. "What was that for?"

"For being the most perfectly imperfect woman. Let's get naked. We have a long night ahead of us."

Chapter Eight

She didn't care.

She didn't care whether he could read or not. She didn't care he'd been lying to everyone his entire life. She did care he'd been a fucking coward but was willing to give him a second chance. He wouldn't waste it.

He pressed her slight form into the mattress, his lips and tongue busily licking and kissing any exposed flesh. He had tugged off her terry cloth robe and she was only wearing a nightshirt underneath. His hand wandered up her silky thigh to play with the edge of the elastic on her panties.

She was wriggling and making sexy sounds in the back of her throat, and it was driving him wild. His cock was hard and pressing against the fly of his jeans, his heart pounding out of control. Only this one tiny woman could get his motor running this fast and this hard. Other women paled in comparison. Hell, there wasn't even a comparison. Leah blew all of them away easily.

He lifted up off her and pulled his T-shirt over his head, tossing it away, before tugging at his button fly. She was propped up on her elbows, watching as he slid his jeans off his legs and kicked them aside. She was smiling and he could see her nipples, hard and pointed, through the thin, white cotton of her nightshirt.

"Like what you see?"

He couldn't believe how vulnerable he felt. Woman usually came on to him, not the other way around. He wanted her to like what she was seeing. To his relief she giggled.

"What I've seen so far, very much. Am I going to see any more?"

So much for the shy, bookish young woman he'd seen in public. In the bedroom, she was teasing and sultry.

He hooked his thumbs in the waistband of his boxers. "Definitely." He shoved the material over his erect cock and tossed them away. His dick was painfully hard and throbbing. He flashed back to seeing Leah on her knees in front of Justin and wondered if he could convince her to do the same for him. It had been an incredibly erotic sight that had tortured him every night since.

"I saw you that first night."

Leah licked her lips as she stared at him. "You saw me when?"

He stepped closer and she reached out to run her fingers down his cock, wrenching a groan from his lips. Her hand felt like heaven.

"The first night when you were with Justin. You were on your knees in front of him. You took his cock in your mouth. I wanted it to be me."

She shook her head. "It could have been, Linc. I would have welcomed you that night even though you hurt me. I thought I saw something out of the corner of my eye. It must have been you."

Her fingers continued exploring him, her palm cupping his balls. His breath was coming in short pants and it was hard to talk.

"It was me. I was coming to join you."

Her hand halted and her expression was sad. "Why didn't you? It was wonderful, but something was missing without you."

"I saw you and you looked so sexy and beautiful. I knew I couldn't hide my secret from you and it scared me."

Leah rose to her knees on the mattress, pressing kisses on his chest and sending lightning straight to his aching cock.

"You hid your secret from everyone."

He pulled her head back and looked deep into her soft brown eyes. "I knew I couldn't hide it from you. You were too smart, and your eyes saw everything. I knew you would see right through me. Believe me, if I thought I could have hid it from you, I would have tried. I wanted to be with you just as much as Justin did."

"You're with me now. What are you going to do with me?"

He pressed her back onto the mattress, insinuating himself between her thighs. He started tugging at her tiny panties until they were sliding down her legs.

"I'm going to eat this pretty, pink pussy. Feel free to scream my name."

* * * *

"Linc!"

She cried out his name at the first touch of his warm tongue on her pussy. She grabbed the sheets, crumpling them in her clenched fists as his mouth tortured her. He ran his tongue through every fold, every corner of her cunt except where she needed him the most. She was ready to beg when he finally lightly brushed her clit with the flat of his tongue, sending shivers of pleasure through her. Her pussy responded by raining honey onto his face and tongue.

He held her there on the edge, playing with her clit but not giving her the pressure she needed to climax. She moaned and panted, her entire body strung as tight as a bow, waiting for release.

He lifted his head and kissed her inner thigh. "Come for me, Leah."

His mouth closed over her clit this time, giving her the firm suckling she needed to soar. He sent her flying, her body suffused with pleasure and heat. He kept her in the clouds until she was too exhausted to continue, her body floating back to earth with a sigh of satisfaction. She let her muscles relax, releasing her death grip on the bedcovers, her eyes closed in languor.

His mouth kissed a path up her sensitized skin, over her belly, to her lips. She tasted herself on him and then she tasted only Linc. His lips and tongue warm, igniting her arousal all over again. She tore her lips away, both of their breathing ragged.

"Fuck me."

He pulled her nightshirt over her head. "I intend to. How do you like it, baby? Hard and fast or soft and slow?"

She ran her fingers through the silky hair on his chest and pulled his head down for another toe-curling kiss.

"I like it both ways. Let's start out hard and slow, then work up to hard and fast."

His grin was wicked, his dark eyes almost black with arousal. "Love the way you think. Are you ready for me?"

She pressed herself against his hard cock. It was hot and pulsing against her.

"I'm ready. Very ready."

He leaned forward and dragged his goatee over her nipple, sending arrows of pleasure straight to her clit. It immediately stiffened, standing at attention, begging for more. He granted its request, lapping at it with his tongue and nipping it with his teeth.

She dug her fingers into his back. "Fuck me now, Linc. I can't wait."

He turned his attention to the other begging nipple. She moaned at the rasp of his facial hair against the pebbled nub.

"Most women like more foreplay. You don't want me to keep playing with you?"

He was teasing her now, a smile playing on his lips as he worried her nipple between his lips. Her pussy burned and honey dripped down her thighs.

"I need you now." She raked her nails down his back in frustration as he sucked her nipple into his mouth, raking the sides with his teeth. She cried out with want and need.

"Give it to me, Linc. I need it now."

He pulled away and she almost grabbed and pulled him back, but he reached into his jeans pocket and pulled out a condom, quickly sheathing himself. He was about the same size as Justin. Maybe an inch shorter, but he was wider in girth. She felt a moment of doubt she could take him. She'd barely been able to take Justin the first time, and Linc was going to be a challenge.

He must have recognized her expression changing and stopped, hovering over her.

"Are you okay, baby? Have you changed your mind?"

She shook her head. "No. I'm just a little nervous." She pointed to his chest and then back at her own. "You're big. I'm little."

He leaned down and let his lips play with hers. "If you can take Justin, you can take me. We'll fit just fine."

He suddenly rolled her over so she was on top, straddling him. "You've got the reins, Leah. Take your time. Do whatever feels good."

She scooted down. "I've never been on top before."

He wrapped his large hands around her hips and pulled her closer, his cock nestled in her slit. "It's like being on the bottom, but you're higher up."

She rolled her eyes at his attempt at a joke. "I'm being serious here. I've never been on top before."

"Take me inside of you as slowly as you need to, then ride me like a cowgirl. Did you ever want to be a cowgirl?"

She placed the head of his cock inside her and started impaling herself a centimeter at a time. "No. I wanted to be Amelia Earhart at one point." The last word came out in a hiss. His cock felt delicious in her cunt and she wanted to savor the feeling of being stretched wide by every luscious inch of it. She paused, letting her muscles get accustomed to his girth, before continuing to lowering herself. By the time he was all the way in, she was ready to ride. In this position, his cock was pressing on her G-spot and she was already halfway to orgasm.

"This feels so good. I think I like being on top."

Linc laughed, but it sounded slightly choked. "I knew you would. It rubs all the right spots, doesn't it, baby?"

It did indeed. She moved up and down, slowly at first, then faster as she gained confidence. Each stroke sent frissons of pleasure to every corner of her body. Fire licked her veins and she was lost to the passion. She braced her hands on his chest, swiveling her hips, experimenting with shorter and longer movements.

She felt his fingers flex on her hips. His eyes were closed, his jaw tight. He was holding back while she played. She leaned down and kissed his lips, whispering in his ear. "It's time, lover."

She gasped when he pressed a thumb to her swollen clit. The pressure was exactly what she needed, and she sped up, needing to go over the cliff. A few more strokes and she screamed his name as her orgasm hit her, almost knocking her sideways. Pleasure ran through her body like waves on the shore. It was liquid fire and she let herself burn, reveling in the heat they'd created together. He lifted his hips, slamming into her one last time before he, too, climaxed. She felt his cock jerk inside of her and then they collapsed in a heap of sweaty, sated flesh.

She licked at his salty skin as she listened to his heart pound under her ear, galloping in time with her own. She was loath to admit she hadn't thought sex could be equally amazing with both Justin and Linc. Her past sexual experiences hadn't encouraged the feeling. She was wrong. It had been as pleasurable as when she was with Justin, but different.

Justin was more playful, while Linc more serious. Even when he had moved her to the top, he had never really given up control. His hands had never left her, helping her move up and down, side to side in a rhythm that drove them both wild. Linc was her bad boy, with his dark hair and eyes, and that goatee which she had never liked on any man before. But after he had played with her nipples, she liked his a whole bunch. Justin was her golden boy, always easygoing and happy, even in bed. He liked to play in the bedroom, proposing games of tag or truth or dare to heighten the anticipation. The men were an intoxicating mixture of yin and yang. She was one lucky woman.

He eased her to her back and pulled away. "I've got to take care of the condom, baby. Don't move."

She didn't want to move. She felt delightfully boneless, her muscles limp. She pulled the covers over her nude body and snuggled under the warm covers, already missing his body heat. She was a native Floridian, and anything under seventy degrees was freezing.

"I went and grabbed a couple of bottles of water from the kitchen. Are you thirsty?"

She sat up, suddenly feeling parched. "Yes, I am. You take good care of me."

His expression was serious. "I always will. I know I hurt you. You could have made me beg and grovel and still not given me a chance."

She wanted him smiling again. "I was planning to, you know. I pictured it. But, after what you told me, it didn't seem right." She shook her finger at him playfully. "I will, however, make you toe the line. Both Justin and Jillian told me to make sure that both of you treat me well. I've decided not to take any crap from either of you. From anyone, as a matter of fact."

"If my being an asshole was a catalyst for this, I guess something good came from it. You're right. Justin and I need to treat you like a princess."

He'd misunderstood. "No, I only meant you should treat me well. I don't need to be some kind of princess. I'm not the princessey type, really." She pointed to the top of her head. "See? No tiara. No self-respecting princess would be without a tiara. I'm just me, and that's plenty good enough."

He stroked her hair, smoothing the strands behind her ear. "I'll have to work on some kind of tiara. You should definitely be a princess."

"Princesses don't wear glasses." She grabbed her glasses from the nightstand and slid them on her face.

He leaned forward and kissed the tip of her nose. "This one does."

She twisted the top off the bottle and took a long swallow, the cool water sliding down her throat. She frowned as the doorbell rang insistently. Linc glanced at the clock. It was near midnight.

"Are you expecting company?"

She shook her head and shrugged into a robe while Linc started to pull on his pants.

"You can't answer my door. You need to stay here."

Linc rolled his eyes and finished buttoning his fly. "Whoever is coming to your door at midnight isn't here to sell you encyclopedias. I'm going to the door with you."

She sighed and headed for the front door. It was probably a mistake anyway. She'd never had anyone ring her doorbell this late at night. They were probably looking for a neighbor. She peered out the peephole and smiled before pulling open the door.

"Justin! What a surprise. Are you here for me or Linc?"

"Both of you." Justin stepped in and took in Linc's state of dress or in this case, undress. "I got your message from Cheryl. I came here to make sure you didn't hurt Leah again. Looks like things have worked out okay."

Linc came to her side and put his arm around her shoulders, pulling her close. "We talked and this generous woman has decided to give me a chance to make things up to her."

A slow grin spread across Justin's face. "It's about damn time." He started plucking open the buttons on his shirt. "Let's all head into the bedroom."

Linc led the way with Justin right behind him. "Wait, both of you. Don't I get a say in this?"

They both stopped and turned. Justin had an anxious expression. "Don't you want to be with both of us? We want you so much, honey."

She scowled. "Of course, I do." In fact, the thought of being with both of them was already firing up her engines. "I just want to make sure my wishes aren't ignored. I get to make decisions, too."

Linc nodded, his lips twitching. "Leah baby, would you let us both make love to you tonight?"

She started walking toward the bedroom. "Yes. I read in a book about having sex in the 'roasting spit' position. Can we do that one?"

Chapter Nine

Holy Mary Mother of God, this woman surprised him on a daily basis. Leah seemed quiet, even shy around people. *Fuck, when you get to know her, she's a wild woman.* Justin was determined to show her how much he appreciated the wanton streak she displayed with him.

And now Linc.

He couldn't even put into words how grateful he was Linc finally came around. This last week, Justin had been falling hard for Leah, and if Linc wasn't on board, Justin was facing going his own way. It was something that would have been unthinkable before, but he wasn't going to lose this wonderful woman. She was too special. He'd dated enough women to know there was a difference with Leah.

Linc lifted Leah into his arms and carried her into the bedroom, laughing. It was good to see Linc happy again. He'd been miserable lately.

"If you want the roasting spit, then Justin and I will give it to you. It's not like we won't enjoy it."

Linc set her down on the carpet and started working on the ties of her robe while Justin shucked his clothes as quickly as possible. His cock was already inflating at the mere thought of making love to his beautiful woman.

Leah looked like a tiny pixie, her body so slim and her hair long and shiny. Yep, a tiny, naked pixie. He tossed his shirt and started working on his pants.

She backed onto the bed, already mussed from her lovemaking with Linc. "Will you spank me and pull my hair, too? That sounds exciting."

He and Linc exchanged glances, both of them grinning from ear to ear. Leah was never boring, that was sure. It was going to be a hell of a lot of fun showing her the fun they could have together in bed. She seemed open-minded and playful. Justin had already initiated her into a game of tag before bed last night. He'd chased her through the upstairs, revving their adrenaline, before the main event. It had been a wild night.

Justin chuckled. "If that's what you want, I'm more than happy to do it." Leah started to get on her hands and knees, but Linc stopped her.

"Not yet. Let's get you begging for some cock first."

He and Linc stretched out on either side of her, running their hands over her satiny-soft skin. It felt right having Linc here with him. He knew it was something many people wouldn't understand, but he didn't care. They were meant to share this woman.

"Isn't her skin soft, Linc? And her pretty pink nipples are begging to be sucked."

His palm glided over her stomach and then her breasts. She was already starting to close her eyes from the double dose of pleasure she was getting from both of them.

"They're small. I'm not very curvy or anything."

He cupped them, his tongue dipping to tease a nipple. Linc was doing the same to her other hardening peak. "They're perfect for our mouths and tongues. The perfect size. See how Linc can fit your nipple into his mouth? I'm going to do the same."

They were sucking and licking on her breasts, her slim body writhing, her breath coming in pants. Justin could see the pearls of honey on the curls between her legs. He reached down and swirled his finger around her clit, making her shiver and moan.

"That's it, honey. Don't hold back. Show us how you feel when we touch you."

Her eyes were closed and she licked her lips, letting her head loll back. He slipped first one, then two fingers inside her warm, wet pussy. Her muscles tightened on him and he hooked his fingers to rub her sweet spot, knowing how much she loved it.

Her whole body trembled as she hovered on the brink of her orgasm. He gave Linc a signal and they both went to work on her nipples while he sped up the strokes with his fingers, brushing her clit with his thumb. Leah froze for a moment, her body going taut before she cried out their names. Her back arched and her cunt clamped down on his fingers, cream raining on his hand.

She rode his fingers until she came down, gasping, her lids fluttering open to look at them dazedly. Linc gave her a long kiss before tweaking a nipple.

"Hands and knees. Time to get fucked."

* * * *

Leah was still quivering from the mind-blowing orgasm her men had given her. She had known being with two men would be amazing, but nothing had prepared her for the reality. There weren't words to describe all the sensations she was feeling at once. Their hands and mouths were everywhere and her body had drank in all the pleasure they had to give.

She moved to her hands and knees, Justin pushing her thighs wide apart, Linc near her head. His hard cock was mere inches from her face and she gave the head a lick, tasting his sweet and salty pre-cum. He hissed and pointed to Justin.

"Give her a smack on the ass for being a naughty little girl."

Before she could protest, Justin's large hand landed on her bottom and she jumped at the sharp contact. She was about to turn around and tell him he had spanked her too hard when the pain turned into a heat spreading to her pussy and clit. She wriggled her ass, wanting more.

Justin chuckled. "She likes it. I thought she would. Don't worry, honey. You'll get all you can handle from me and Linc. We love nothing better than to spank a cute little rear end like yours all night. Eventually, we'll fuck it, too."

His finger trailed down into her ass crack and circled her tight rosette. "Would you like that? Do you want us to fuck your ass, honey?"

She was already climbing toward orgasm again. Linc's fingers had reached under her and were playing with her nipples while Justin's finger was teasing her back door.

"Yes," she gasped. "I want you to do whatever you want. Spank it, fuck it. Whatever."

Justin leaned over and nipped at her shoulder. "We'll do both those things. The fucking will need to wait for another night, but it will happen."

He leaned down and grabbed his pants and pulled out a condom. "You want a spit roast, huh? Do you want the Eiffel Tower as well?"

She'd never heard of the Eiffel Tower.

"What's that?"

Linc fisted his cock so it was right under her nose. He had a big grin on his face and she was once more taken aback by how handsome he looked when he was smiling.

"It's when the two guys high-five over the woman at the end."

She turned back to give Justin a dirty look. "Don't you dare."

Justin rolled on the condom with a smirk. "I wouldn't do it even if you double-dog dared me."

"Justin?"

"Yes, honey?"

"I double-dog dare you to spank and fuck me."

He was deep inside her in one hard thrust, taking her breath away. "Dare accepted. What about Linc?"

She looked up into Linc's dark eyes, not cold and lifeless this time. They were hot with arousal, the golden ring around the pupil glowing. She took a deep breath.

"I double-dog dare you to pull my hair and fuck my face."

"I thought you wanted Justin to pull your hair."

Smart-ass.

"I'm about to change my mind about both of you, sending you home with blue balls."

They both laughed. Justin pressed a kiss to the ass cheek he'd spanked. "Give us hell, honey."

Linc's cock was pressing her lips for entry and she opened wide to let him all the way in. He was big and her mouth was small but she stretched her jaws wide to take as much as she could. He patted her cheek.

"Easy. Don't try and take it all."

His fingers wound through her thick hair, anchoring her head into place. His other hand cupped her jaw gently, but firmly, tucking a stray strand of hair behind her ear. Justin's hands were gripping her hips, starting to take shallow thrusts. She loved the feeling of being under their control, her honey dripping from her pussy in response. She had so many things she'd read about she was going to want to try. Tonight was only the beginning. She was going to talk to them about tying her up next time.

Linc had taken control and was thrusting slowly in and out of her mouth, the ridges of his cock running over her tongue. She relaxed her jaw and tried to take him deeper, the head of his cock bumping the back of her throat. She swallowed on him, dragging a groan from his lips.

One glance up and she could see he was deep in the pleasure zone, his head thrown back, his teeth bared, the cords of his neck standing out. It was unbearably sexy to be watching him this way while she sucked on his thick cock. Every time she flicked her tongue on the underside of his dick, she could see his reaction in his expression.

Smack!

She jumped when Justin's hand came down on her ass cheek, sending a streak of heat straight to her cunt. His cock was stroking deeper into her pussy and she pressed back with each thrust, trying to take him as deeply as she could.

She was being fucked hard from both ends and her arousal rose with every stroke of their hard cocks. It was dirty, raunchy, and she wanted to experience it every day for the rest of her life. She'd never felt so much pleasure at one time. Making love to both her men made her feel complete.

Justin was spanking her hard and she kept arching her back, inviting his punishment. This was what she had fantasized about so many times. It was a million trillion times better in reality. She wanted him to spank her harder and faster. Each time his hand came down on her bottom, her whole body tingled and quaked.

Linc's fingers tightened in her hair. "I'm ready to blow, baby."

She tightened her lips around his cock and flitted her tongue back and forth, giving him butterfly kisses on his dick. He groaned her name and she could feel him swell inside her mouth as his cum jetted into her throat. She drank every hot drop until he had nothing left to give her. He leaned back and reached under her, playing with her nipples, twisting them and giving her a bite of pain.

"Like that, baby? Do you want me to stop?"

She could barely breathe, let alone speak, but she couldn't let him stop what he was doing. She shook her head as Justin pounded her pussy hard and fast, her ass on fire from her spanking. She was so close to coming she wanted to scream. Linc seem to recognize her frustration and slid a hand down to her clit, rubbing circles around the swollen nub.

She went off like a firecracker on the Fourth of July.

Her entire body shattered, pieces of her soul flying everywhere. She screamed as the pleasure grew so strong it was almost painful. It battered at her body, giving her no quarter. Her pussy tightened on Justin's cock and it triggered his climax. He rammed into her one last time, his cock jerking as he came, expletives falling from his lips. They all fell into a heap on the bed, breathing ragged, sticky with sweat and her honey.

Finally, Justin extricated himself from the tangle of arms and legs, heading to the bathroom to take care of the condom. She rolled over so she was tucked into Linc's arms. He stroked her back and ran his fingers through her hair.

"I've dreamed about all of us together. Thank you for giving me a chance, Leah."

"Thank you for telling me the truth. When are you going to tell Justin?"

His fingers moved down to her bottom, rubbing the sore, hot cheeks.

"I'll tell him tomorrow. He's going to be pissed as hell that I kept this from him."

"He's going to be hurt more than angry. He may not like you very much for a while."

"That's his right. I can't blame him. I'll let him take a swing at me if it will help."

Leah giggled. "You sound like my brother, Gabe. He said he'd let my cousin, Jason, punch him. I'm not really sure what it solves though."

"Doesn't solve anything, but it makes everyone feel better. Sounds like your brother and cousin have some history."

"They have some things to work out. They will though. Despite their ups and downs, they're as close as brothers. Just like you and Justin."

She could hear the padding of Justin's feet as he returned to the bedroom. He slid in beside her and she luxuriated in having both her men beside her as she slept. She relaxed and let sleep overtake her, feeling safe and warm in their arms.

* * * *

Leah was sleeping deeply between them, her breathing slow, her face serene. Justin reached over and nudged Linc's shoulder. He knew

Linc wasn't asleep yet. He lifted his head.

"What?" Linc's voice soft, barely a whisper, to keep from waking up Leah.

"What did you say to Leah to get her to forgive you? You did apologize for hurting her, didn't you?"

Justin didn't want this to be a temporary reconciliation between the two. He wanted the air to be well and truly cleared.

Linc's lips twisted. "Of course. Several times. She accepted my apology. I told her the truth. I told her why I'd been holding back."

Justin shifted so Leah was leaning back against his chest. "Are you planning to tell me why or is it going to be one of those mysteries of the universe?"

Linc didn't answer for a minute. "I'm going to tell you, but not right now. You're probably going to be angry with me when I do and I don't want Leah in between us."

"The only thing I care about is that we're all three together." He didn't want to ask, but he couldn't stop himself.

"Is it another woman? Have you been involved with someone else?"

"Fuck no. The last time I slept with a woman was the last time you slept with a woman, and that was months ago. No, this is about me."

Justin couldn't honestly think of anything Linc could say that would make him angry. Linc was more than a brother to him. Whatever he had to say, Justin would have to learn to deal with one way or another. There wasn't a choice. Not having Linc in his life wasn't an option. He'd grown accustomed to Linc's ugly mug and off-key singing voice.

"You don't have to tell me. I don't really care what it was about. It doesn't matter now anyway."

The moonlight spilled in through the window and threw shadows along the walls. He saw Linc's shadow move before he actually saw Linc sit up. "You need to know this. It does matter. I should have told you years ago. I shouldn't have kept it a secret from you."

Justin shrugged even though no one could see the motion. "If this is something from the past, then it really doesn't matter. If it hasn't mattered all these years, then it doesn't matter at all now."

He heard Linc's chuckle. "I'm going to remind you of this conversation tomorrow when you want to kick my ass all over Plenty."

Justin closed his eyes. "I told you it doesn't matter. I trust you. Now that whatever it was is behind us, we can move forward. Isn't Leah amazing? I'm falling for her, Linc."

"She is amazing. I've only had one night with her but my feelings are strong. I can see she's the type of woman we've been waiting for. I promise I won't fuck up again."

Leah stirred in her sleep and they both quieted immediately. She settled again, and Justin let pictures of the future dance in his head. He smiled. He knew this mood well. He would be up all night writing lyrics to a new song. A song for Leah.

Chapter Ten

The smell of garlic and tomato sauce from Charlie's kitchen filled the air and Leah breathed in the heavenly scent. She was totally starving. She and her men had spent the last few hours working up an appetite by doing naughty and salacious things in their bedroom. They'd made her come so many times she thought her pussy might fall out of her body at one point. Luckily, she was completely intact and ready for another round after their date tonight.

They'd gotten into the habit of going to Charlie's on Friday nights before heading to bingo, and then on to their nightclub. The last three weeks has been the best in her life, hands down. Even Linc, with his normally serious attitude, had lightened up. He smiled much more easily now and seemed more relaxed, less on edge. She knew he wasn't worried about everyone finding out about his reading problem. He'd told Justin, and Justin had gone through several emotions, including disbelief, anger, and hurt, before getting to reconciliation. He'd immediately arranged for a specialist in Jacksonville to evaluate Linc for a reading disability.

The verdict had been severe dyslexia. He had both a phonological deficiency paired with deficient naming speed. It made reading incredibly difficult for him and the doctor had told them that in most undiagnosed cases the child would give up trying to learn. Most mainstream teaching methods simply weren't effective in these cases. Linc needed alternative methods to learn to read better.

Linc worked with the doctor and found strategies which helped him. Leah learned the strategies and now they worked together three to four days a week. His reading had already improved a great deal and he was starting to write her notes, too. It had boosted his confidence, but he kept telling her learning to read wasn't what made him feel good about himself. What made it was how she didn't care if he could read or not.

"I'm hungry. You're wearing me out, honey." Justin had a teasing smile on his face as he perused the menu. It was really a formality. They always ordered the same thing.

"You've got nerve. I could swear the last time was your idea, and the time before that, Linc's."

Linc raised his eyebrows. "And you were just lying there thinking about being a good girl? I don't think so. You were being naughty so we would spank you."

She pouted. "You didn't, though. I love it when you spank me." She leaned forward. "Can we do it tonight? You know, the other stuff I want to do?"

She kept her voice down even though the restaurant was loud and the jukebox was rocking in the corner. Justin and Linc exchanged a glance.

Linc put down the menu. "We'll do anything within reason to make you happy. Are you sure about this?"

Leah nodded. She'd been thinking about it for a couple of weeks. "I'm very sure. Does it not turn you on?"

Justin laughed. "It turns us on, all right. Very on. My dick got hard as a brick when I read that book you gave me. Then I got turned on all over again when I ordered what we needed online. I can't wait to see you cuffed to the bed. We're going to tie you up and spank you tonight."

She shivered with excitement. She trusted them to take good care of her, and of course, bring all her fantasies to life. After all, they were fantasy men.

Linc waved to someone over her shoulder and she twisted in her chair to see who it was. Two tall men with broad shoulders were smiling and heading toward their table. Both were handsome, muscular, and garnering more than their share of attention. Every female head in the place swiveled to follow their trek across the restaurant. Leah couldn't help but be glad there were two new men in town who could keep some of the women who used to chase Justin and Linc busy.

Justin pulled another chair from an adjoining table. "Sit down and join us. Hell, Logan, Meyer, what are you doing in Plenty? I thought you never left Los Angeles? It's been forever since we've seen you, man."

The dark-haired man with the ponytail smiled, a dimple appearing on his right cheek. "It was a year and a half ago. You were playing the Palladium in London. We did the background checks for the security team and the press."

Justin shook his head. "Man, time flies. I'll ask the question again. What the hell brings you to Plenty?"

The man pointed at Linc. "We're doing some work for Linc. He didn't tell you about it?"

Justin quirked an eyebrow. "Linc is full of surprises lately." He put his arm around Leah. "Hey, first I want you to meet our girlfriend, Leah." He pointed to the man with the ponytail. "That's Logan Farraday." Justin pointed to the quiet, unsmiling man with short dark hair and intense blue eyes. "That's Meyer Smith, his partner. This is Leah Holt. She owns the bookstore in town."

Leah smiled at both of them. "It's very nice to meet you. Welcome to Plenty. I hope you enjoy your stay."

Logan grinned. "*Our* girlfriend, huh? I see you finally got what you wanted when you moved here. I remember both of you talking about it."

Linc sipped his drink. "Quietly talking about it, you mean. The only reason we told you is because you told us first."

Logan chuckled. "I believe we were doing tequila shots after the concert, celebrating the end of another successful tour. Damn, that stuff should be outlawed. It's like truth serum in a bottle." He turned to Leah. "We admitted to them we had always wanted a woman in our life." He put his arm around Meyer and gave the man a loving look. "Meyer and I are partners in all ways, but we still enjoy female company."

Leah had seen way too many alternate-lifestyle relationships growing up in Plenty to be shocked.

"You came to the right town. One of my friends married and recently had a son with her two men. They were a couple for fifteen years before they found her. They're all very happy."

Meyer finally gave her a tentative smile. "Most people aren't as open-minded as you seem."

"Plenty's a very open-minded town. We try not to judge people. Besides, I'm dating two men. I don't have much room to talk. My parents were in a ménage and so are many people in this town. To me it's normal."

The two men ordered beers from the passing waitress. Meyer turned back to her, a serious expression on his face. "Please don't think I'm being nosy, but poly relationships aren't the norm in LA. We've never actually seen a successful relationship with two bisexual men and one woman. You say your friends are in this sort of a relationship. It's working? Are they happy? Do they argue or get jealous?"

Logan frowned. "Don't put her on the spot, babe."

Leah shook her head. "No, it's okay. I don't think Becca, Mark, and Travis would mind me saying how freakin' deliriously happy they are. Mark and Travis look at her like she hung the moon. They're so proud of their newborn son, Noah. Becca adores both her husbands. Everyone brings something different to the relationship." She nodded at Justin and Linc. "Just like in our relationship. But the dynamic is different." She laughed as Meyer's face lit up. He was an extremely handsome man. They both were.

"I'd love to meet them while we're here. Do you think they would mind talking about things with us?"

"I can ask, if you like."

Meyer and Logan both nodded excitedly, grins on their faces. They both looked very happy and she was glad she'd been able to assure them their relationship desires, while not common, weren't unheard of. She wondered if they were going to try and live a ménage in Los Angeles. How ménage friendly the city was she didn't know.

Linc pushed his empty beer bottle away. "Let's get down to business. What brings you here and how in the hell did you find us tonight?" He laughed. "I know you guys are good, but fuck, do you have us under surveillance?"

Logan thanked the waitress for the beer before turning back to Linc. "We found out a few things about your Bobbi Blackwell. We were in Palm Beach visiting Meyer's parents and decided to stop off here to talk to you about what we've found so far. It's been too long since we've hung out. As for finding you tonight, that was easy. We went to your new nightclub and the people there were more than happy to tell us that Friday night was date night. Charlie's for pizza, bingo, then back to the club."

Justin sipped his ice water. He was the designated driver tonight. "Are you going to give us a rash about bingo? It's not very LA, I suppose."

Meyer looked around. "Fuck no. I think this little town is great. It's nice to get out of La La Land. I get tired of the West Coast, personally. Good to have a break now and then. Maybe we can join you at bingo later."

The waitress came up to the table for their order and the conversation paused. After she left, Linc asked, "So, what have you found out about Bobbi?"

Logan leaned back in his chair. "She's broke. Busted. Her husband of a couple of months cleaned her out and ran off with his secretary."

Leah didn't know who Bobbi was but her men looked shocked. "Who's Bobbi?"

"Bobbi is a concert promoter who's trying to get me to come out of retirement for some big tour," Justin explained.

"Are you going to do it?" The thought of him being gone for months made her heart clench.

"Hell to the no. I'm fucking retired and intend to stay that way. Mr. Suspicious here"—Justin elbowed Linc—"decided to have her investigated when she didn't take no for an answer. I guess now we know why."

Linc played with the silverware. "Are you sure she's broke? When we saw her she didn't look or act broke. Quite the opposite, in fact."

Meyer answered this time. "Very sure. She's dripping in the red. I daresay she's living off whatever credit hasn't been cut off. She's millions in debt and desperate. I talked to some of her so-called friends. She's desperate to hold on to her high-flying lifestyle. That's where you come in, Justin."

"Me? What do I have to do with anything?"

"She needs you to get the sponsors on board. She can't bankroll this thing herself. She needs to be completely underwritten. According to reliable sources, the sponsors won't sign on without you. They don't care what other bands she gets. They want Justin Reynolds, rock star and golden boy."

Justin was really scowling now. "Fuck, I hate it when people call me a golden boy."

Leah rolled her eyes. "If they could hear you snore they'd probably stop calling you that. I doubt any of them want to clean up the kitchen after you make dinner, or pick up your socks and underwear from the bedroom floor and put them in the hamper. Face it, you're a slob."

Logan and Meyer looked speechless but Justin and Linc simply threw back their heads and laughed. Justin winked at her. "This is why I'm crazy about this woman. She doesn't give a rat's ass whether I'm rich and famous. She couldn't be less impressed with me."

If they hadn't had company at dinner, Leah would have told him in no uncertain terms the ways he did impress her. Instead, she gave him a mischievous look that hopefully conveyed her meaning.

"We'll e-mail you the relevant documentation," Logan said. "Wow, that pizza looks delicious."

Charlie dropped off two large pizzas and a basket of her famous garlic breadsticks on the table before bustling off. The place was packed as usual on a Friday night and would be until closing time.

They were quiet while they ate, Logan and Meyer raving about the pizza and complimenting the town. Several people stopped by their table to say hello, especially women who wanted to meet the two new hunks.

"If you wanted to hang around town, I think you could find a woman or two who would be willing to be your third," Leah teased. "I've never had so many female friends feel compelled to say hello to me during dinner."

Logan rubbed his chin. "We were planning to stay in Tampa tonight and fly out tomorrow, but I like it here. I think we might stay for a few days. Do you know where we can get a hotel room around here? One with Wi-Fi. We need it to do our work."

Justin pushed away his empty plate and sighed. "You can stay at our place. We have several bedrooms. You'll have all the privacy you need. Sock- and underwear-free, I promise."

Meyer looked unsure. "We wouldn't want to put you to any trouble."

Linc grabbed the check as it was placed on the table. "No trouble at all. We can drop your luggage at the house after bingo and before we hit the club."

Meyer smiled. "Well, if you're sure, that would be great. Thank you." He reached for the check in Linc's hand. "But please let us get that. You're our client and letting us stay at your place. It's the least we can do."

Linc was about to argue but Logan beat him to it. "Please. We wouldn't feel right about staying with you if we didn't at least pay for dinner."

Linc nodded, handing over the check reluctantly. "This one time. Thank you."

Justin stretched his legs out. "Are we ready to head to bingo then? I'm feeling lucky tonight." Justin tugged her to her feet and grabbed her purse from under the table.

"Sorry, babe. I'm planning to win the big pot tonight. I know just what I want to do with the five hundred bucks."

Linc chuckled. "If you want something, baby, we'll be happy to get it for you."

She shook her head. "No way. I buy my own things."

Justin threw an arm around her as they walked up to the cash register with Logan and Meyer. "Isn't she a gem? I'm a lucky man."

She pulled him down and whispered a few promises in his ear. He was definitely going to get lucky tonight.

* * * *

Meyer grabbed Linc's arm and pulled him away from the others.

"We didn't tell you everything. There's one more thing."

Linc didn't like the look on his old friend's face. It wasn't going to be good.

"Fuck, I'm going to hate this."

Meyer's lips twisted in a grimace. "I talked to a couple of people I guess you could call Bobbi's friends. Shit, even her friends know what a phony she is. Anyway, one of them told me she wasn't going to take no for an answer from Justin. She was going to force him to do the tour."

"Screw her. She can't force Justin to do anything."

"Maybe. The friend seemed to think Bobbi had some sort of evidence that Justin wouldn't want revealed. Something that would compel him to do the tour even if he didn't want to."

Linc was rocked back on his heels. Bobbi was talking about

blackmailing them? She knew Justin's image was a large part of his popularity. He was the golden boy for millions of fans.

"Has Justin done anything you need to worry about? If so, maybe Logan and I can try and cover it up. Make it go away."

Linc shook his head in disbelief. "No. Fuck no. Justin is as squeaky clean in real life as his image. Hell, he barely drinks, never does drugs, and gives generously to charity. Shit, he's even nice to animals. She's bluffing. She's got nothing."

"This friend was convinced Bobbi thinks she has something. If you want, I can check out Justin's past. Maybe she's planning to reveal something about a family member."

Linc shook his head. "No. I won't investigate my best friend. I'll talk to him later tonight and see if he knows anything. His family is pretty mainstream, Middle America stuff. I can't imagine them doing anything that would embarrass Justin."

Meyer nodded. "I just wanted to give you the option. We're old friends and I'd hate to see anything bad happen to either of you."

"I appreciate it. We came here to start a new life out of the spotlight. Things are falling into place."

Linc thought about Leah and how happy they'd all been these last weeks. He didn't want anything to destroy what they were building together.

"I can see how happy you and Justin are. Leah's seems great. I wish Logan and I could find a woman like her. I don't suppose she has a sister or anything?"

Linc laughed. "A brother. A big, mean one. This town is full of beautiful women, however. I'm glad you're going to stay a couple of days. Maybe you'll decide to move here."

Meyer shook his head. "It would take quite a woman to get us to leave the big city. We've spent a lot of years building up our business. Our clientele is made up of some of Hollywood's biggest names."

"Are you happy?"

Meyer's shoulders slumped. "Sometimes. Not enough lately."

Linc slapped him on the back. "My friend Brayden says life is too short to be anything but happy. Think about that."

They headed to catch up to the rest of their group. "I will think about it. Your friend is right."

Linc caught up with Leah and pulled her close. Life was too short. He wouldn't let anything come between him and Leah ever again.

Chapter Eleven

Justin sat back in his chair, relaxed and happy. The nightclub was packed with happy, dancing people, Leah was sitting next to him, talking with Ava and her men, Logan and Meyer were having a great time, and he was getting ready to go onstage to sing a new song. A song he'd written for Leah. He was nervous as usual, never getting over the stage fright which had plagued him throughout his career. Tonight, however, the stakes were higher. He wanted this song to tell Leah what he felt for her. He'd fallen in love with his pretty little bookworm. He hoped she felt the same.

He believed she loved them as well. Her every action and word said she did. She was too honest and forthright to hide her feelings. It was one of the reasons he loved her so much.

Brayden Tyler signaled the waiter for another beer. He, along with his two friends, had moved from New York and started a new life in Plenty. They owned the coffee shop and the martial arts studio and were engaged to Ava Bryant, a nurse originally from Chicago.

"You're singing tonight? We don't get to hear you perform very often."

Justin nodded. "I am singing tonight. I only like to perform when I want to debut some new material and gauge the audience reaction. I have a new song I just wrote."

"I'm sure people will love it," Ava enthused. "I have all your albums."

Justin let his fingers wander higher on Leah's thigh, feeling her shiver in response. "Thank you, but with this song, it only matters what one person thinks."

Leah's soft brown eyes were full of emotion. She leaned close so only he would hear. "Am I the one person?"

Justin snorted. "It sure as hell isn't Linc. I know you don't care about the whole music thing, honey, but I wrote the song for you. I hope you like it."

He chuckled as she started to sniffle. "I already like it. It's the thought, Justin, not the actual song."

"I could have saved myself a lot of time and just thought about writing you a song instead of actually doing it then."

He felt a hand on his shoulder.

"Justin, do you have a minute? It's important." Linc was nodding toward their office. Linc's expression was serious. Justin nodded and made his excuses to the table and Leah, before following Linc upstairs.

Justin closed the door behind him. "What's going on? You don't look too damn happy. Problems with the staff?"

Linc leaned against the window looking down on the club. "Meyer pulled me aside at Charlie's. There was another thing they uncovered in their investigation. Bobbi thinks she had something on you. Some secret so heinous you'll do the tour to make sure it doesn't go public."

Justin shook his head. "There's nothing. You know that. I've lived the last fifteen years with paparazzi following my every move. Nothing was a secret."

Linc straightened up and started pacing the office. "What about your family? Everything okay there?"

"Of course, we were just there at Christmas. They're the most boring family in America, living on the most boring street."

Linc came to a stop in front of him, his expression grim. "I think we need to face the fact she may know about me."

Justin hopped up. "You? What about you? Are you talking about your reading issue? No way. Fuck, I didn't even know until three weeks ago. There's no way Bobbi could know."

Linc shrugged, obviously frustrated. "What else could it be?" He started pacing again. "If she threatens to go public, let the bitch do it. I won't let you get blackmailed into doing something you don't want to do because of my pride."

Justin grabbed Linc's arm. "Stop, man. It's not your job to protect me anymore. We're partners. If it weren't for you, I wouldn't even have a career. I'm not throwing you under the bus to save a career I don't even want anymore."

Linc looked shocked. "You'd go on tour then?"

Justin laughed. "No fucking way. Bobbi's under the impression I care what people think about me. I don't. I want to live my life quietly here in Plenty with Leah and you. End of story. Nothing she has on me would compel me to do something I don't want to do."

Justin swung around when there was a sharp knock on the door. Cheryl opened the door a crack. "The band is ready for you, Justin. Are you still performing tonight?"

"Yeah. Give me five."

The door closed and he put his hand on Linc's shoulder. His best friend needed to stop stressing about this. Justin wasn't worried in the least.

"Forget about Bobbi. She doesn't have any weapons. Now let's get downstairs. We've left Leah alone too long."

Justin headed for the door, but Linc hung back. "Are you coming?"

Linc nodded. "Just in case, I'm going to have Logan and Meyer keep investigating her. I want to know what she has."

Linc would never change, always wanting to be one step ahead of everyone and everything. It's what made him a great manager.

"You do that. I doubt she has anything we care about."

He and Linc headed down the stairs. Linc looked pensive. "I hope you're right, Justin. Bobbi makes me nervous. A desperate person does desperate things."

* * * *

Leah was sitting in the audience, waiting for Justin to come on stage. She hadn't wanted to admit it to him, but she'd never seen him perform, even here at the nightclub. She wasn't much for going out and partying before she met him, and even now she preferred a quiet evening with her two men. They seemed to like it, too.

She'd heard his music. When he'd moved here, she'd purchased some of his songs for her iPod. He had a great voice, and she liked listening to his smoky vocals whether the song was soft and slow or an up-tempo rock song.

Tonight was different. He was singing a song for her. She wasn't sure how she was supposed to act. Was she supposed to rush the stage like a teenage fan girl or act all grateful when he was done? She was a private person and her first instinct had been to beg him to not perform it on stage here in front of everyone. She'd rather hear it when the three of them were alone.

She didn't do it. She could tell it was important to Justin. This relationship wasn't all about her, even though her men often made it seem that way. It was about their needs, too. Tonight she would put Justin first.

Linc pulled out the chair next to her and sat down. "Justin will be on stage in a minute. Are you going to be okay when he sings?"

She frowned. "Are you afraid I'm going to get a case of the vapors like some simpering heroine from an antebellum novel? I can assure you I won't."

Linc laughed at her clipped tone. "Hell no. You're definitely not the fainting type. I only meant are you going to be okay with him singing a song to you in front of all these people? I know don't like being the center of attention. You like your privacy."

Her heart warmed and she cuddled closer to Linc. He really understood her. "I do like my privacy. I can tell this is important to him. I can handle it for one night."

"He won't say the song's for you when he's onstage. He knew you would be mortified if every head in the place swiveled to stare at you. He'll just say he has a new song."

It hasn't occurred to her he might talk about her onstage, and she felt relief and gratitude he wasn't going to do it. He was right. She would be mortified. Mortified and hiding under a table.

"Justin's song is for you?"

Gabe was standing over her, smiling. She pulled him into the seat next to her.

"Shhhh! Keep your voice down. I don't want everyone in Plenty to know my business. Got it?"

Gabe simply laughed and signaled a waitress. "Got it, sis. Damn, you get feistier every day. Justin and Linc are a good influence on you. Hey, Linc." Gabe shook Linc's hand before asking the waitress for a soda.

"Where have you been? I haven't seen you in days it seems like." Leah kept her eyes on the stage where Justin and the band were tuning up.

"I've been back and forth to Orlando, spending time with a friend there and working some with him. You didn't think I came back to Plenty to be a bum and sponge off of you, did you?"

"I can hardly say that, can I? Groceries magically appear, the house gets scrubbed by fairies, and my laundry shows up clean and folded on my dresser. I've never had it so good."

Gabe chuckled. "It's the least I can do. I want to make up the last few years."

She put her hand over his. "You have. I want to see you make up with Jason most of all."

Gabe accepted his drink from the waitress with a smile. "We're working on it, sis. It's going to take some time, but we both want it. You can't erase what happened overnight."

Leah didn't know everything that happened, but knew it had been a nasty blowup between the two of them.

"As long as you two are talking about your feelings, everything will be okay."

Linc almost choked on his beer.

Gabe grinned. "Linc, will you tell my little sister men don't talk about their feelings with other men? We just beat on each other until the feelings don't matter anymore. The only feeling is pain."

Linc coughed and shook his head. "Baby, your brother is right. He and Jason will work it out like men."

Leah snorted. "And take ten times as long to do it. One good conversation and some tears would set this right tonight."

Gabe and Linc looked shocked. "You want me to cry?" Gabe asked. "I'm not going to cry to Jason. Fuck, he'd kick my ass and tell me to man up. He'd be right, too."

Leah shook her head. "Men. Lord save me from all the alpha males in my life. You make everything more difficult than it has to be."

Gabe pointed to the stage. "Looks like one of your alpha males is ready to sing."

The lights went down and the stage was illuminated by spotlights. Justin was smiling and he did look like the golden boy he hated to be called. His blond hair caught the lights, and his tan skin glowed. He was handsome and sexy in an all-American way.

The man next to her was sexy in a sinful, dark way. She rested her head on his shoulder and his arm tightened around her as Justin stood at the microphone.

"The song we're about to perform is new. I hope you like it."

Leah wasn't sure what she had been expecting. If she had been a betting woman, she would have guessed the song to be a ballad. It wasn't by a mile. The band was rocking and Justin was playing his guitar and having fun. The whole band had grins on their faces and she found herself tapping her toes to the beat and smiling at the words.

Kisses sweet, sunshine and wine
I'd never met a girl so fine
You're gonna make me toe the line
You're my world, my life, my star
I had to travel wide and far
You're a woman wise and strong
I've waited for you too damn long
Believe in us, believe in love
Plenty to believe
Plenty to believe
Plenty to believe in

By the time he finished the entire song, Justin was covered in sweat and grinning ear to ear. He winked in her direction and her heart skipped a beat. He hadn't sung her some mushy love song. He'd written her an anthem for what she was becoming and who she wanted to be.

She turned to Linc, who was smiling and relaxed. "Had you heard the song before this?"

He kissed the top of her head. "Yes. I helped him with the lyrics, baby. I do that a lot."

She pulled his lips down to hers, kissing him hard. "Thank you both for my song. I loved it."

"It was mostly Justin. I only helped with a line or two. Just when he gets stuck."

"It doesn't matter who did what. Now let's get out of here."

Linc looked confused. "Where are we going?"

She stood up and tugged at his arm. "I'm taking both of you home. Now."

Justin was suddenly standing right next to her. "What's going on?"

"Good, you're here. Can you leave Cheryl in charge?"

Justin nodded. "Sure we can. What's the hurry?"

She glanced over her shoulder and was relieved to see Gabe was deep in conversation with Brayden and Falk. She turned back to her men.

"I'm in a hurry because I want to get you both home." She kept her voice down so only they could hear. "I want both of you making love to me as soon as possible."

Linc caught the attention of a passing waitress. "Tell Cheryl she's in charge. We're heading home." He smiled. "We're heading home. I like the way that sounds."

Justin nodded. "Me, too. I say we get our bookworm there and never let her go."

Chapter Twelve

The song seemed to have worked. Leah had dragged the two of them all the way home as fast as legally possible. Luckily, they didn't live far from the club. Linc had scooped her up in his arms and Justin was pulling her shoes off as they walked in the front door.

"Wait!" Leah held up her hand. "You didn't close the door. You don't want any critters taking up residence in your house."

"Our house," Justin corrected, kicking the door shut with his foot and sliding his hand under her dress and tugging at her panties. She giggled and turned pink.

"Behave yourself until we get in the bedroom. The drapes are wide open."

Linc laughed and carried her into the bedroom, tossing her on the bed. "We live in the middle of nowhere, baby. Unless we have a stalker, no one's going to see. We could have sex outside and no one would be around."

Linc's eyes lit up and Leah looked horrified at the suggestion. "Uh-uh, I am not having sex outdoors. It's fucking cold out there."

Justin nodded. "She's right. Too cold, even in Florida. We'll have to wait for summer."

Leah shook her head. "No way. Mosquitoes would eat our private parts. There are certain places I don't want to be itchy, and my private parts are at the top of the list."

Justin went for her panties again, tugging them down her flailing legs and tossing them across the room. She was only pretending to struggle. She was giggling the entire time. He pressed a kiss to her inner thigh. "I believe you said something about eating private parts?"

Her legs fell open in invitation. "I did say something, didn't I?"

He pressed her thighs apart, breathing in the scent of her arousal. Her pussy was already swollen and wet, ready for him to do whatever he pleased. She had a few fun requests tonight, but then so did he. He liked to play games in the bedroom and he had a good one planned.

He ran his finger down her wet slit and pressed inside of her tight cunt. Her muscles contracted around him and added a second digit, finding her sweet spot. Her head fell back and her lips parted with a sigh when he licked her clit. Linc was pushing the top of her dress down so her breasts were exposed and playing with her nipples, visibly hard through the sheer lace.

As sexy as her bra and panties were, Justin was going to have a talk with her about wearing undergarments at all. They simply got in the way.

He traced the folds of her pussy, licking up the honey she made. Her flavor was sweet and musky and he could have stayed down there all night, except he wanted to play his game. He ran his tongue around and around her clit, feeling it swell even more under his tongue.

"Come for me, honey."

Between his mouth on her clit, and Linc's on her nipples, Leah didn't stand a chance holding back. She screamed and trembled as he tortured her little nub until she was gasping and begging for respite. He sat up and waggled his eyebrows.

"Only the beginning. I've got a surprise for you I hope you'll like."

Her eyes were closed but she had a satisfied smile on her face. "Another one? The song was the first. What's the second?"

"Linc, lift her off the bed for a minute."

Linc chuckled, but did as Justin asked. He wasn't sure if Linc knew what was coming, but he knew Linc would play along. He may act more serious than Justin, but Linc had a devilish streak a mile wide.

When Linc had Leah in his arms, Justin tore back the comforter and blankets, leaving only the sheets.

"Ta-da!"

Linc started laughing so hard, Justin thought he might drop Leah. Leah looked amazed and then started laughing with him. He knew she'd love this. She was as playful as he was.

He pulled the game spinner out of the drawer in the bedside table.

"A game of Twister. Loser gets a spanking and tied to the bed."

* * * *

Her playful Justin had replaced the usual bedsheets with sheets imprinted with a Twister game. It was sexy and fun and she couldn't wait to play. It was too bad losing had such a great prize. She didn't like losing much, but if she received a spanking it wouldn't seem like a defeat.

Justin popped open the button on his jeans and Linc did the same. "Strip, baby. This game is Naked Twister."

She didn't hesitate, pulling her already disheveled dress off and tossing it on a chair. She knelt on the bed, watching her men's bodies revealed inch by inch.

Damn, they look hot.

Justin was her golden god with his blond hair, blue eyes, and muscular build. Linc was her pirate with his dark hair and eyes, goatee, and wide shoulders leading down to a washboard stomach. She leaned forward and licked at his abs, feeling the muscles tense underneath her tongue and his cock jerk in reaction. He stepped away quickly.

"Easy. We have a game to play. You don't want to disappoint Justin, do you?"

What she really wanted to do was trace the ridges on their bellies one by one with her tongue, but the game would come first.

She sat back on her heels. "So who gets to spin first?"

Justin pushed the spinner toward her. "Ladies first, honey."

She spun and smiled. "Right hand red. My favorite color."

Within ten minutes, they were laughing, tangled and twisted together on the gigantic bed. It was easy to see she was going to lose. The men had a huge advantage with their long arms and legs, not to mention a foot of height on her. She could barely stretch from one side of the bed to another, only her toes on "left foot green."

Justin spun a "right hand blue" and reached under her, brushing her nipples before settling on the circle. Linc spun "right hand yellow" and let his fingers trail through her already wet pussy, circling her clit, on the way to their destination.

"No fair. You're cheating."

Linc chuckled. "All's fair in love and Twister. You can cheat, too, if you want. We won't mind."

Her stomach fluttered when he used the word *love*. Did he love her? Did Justin?

She spun a "right foot red" and groaned inwardly. It was all the way on the other side of the bed. She stretched out her leg, inching her toes toward the red disc. No way could she even try to touch or torture her men without falling on her ass. Already, she had her legs stretched wide, leaning forward on her hands, with her pussy in the air for all to see. Justin was behind her and he leaned over and nibbled on her ass cheek, causing her to almost topple over, her balance precarious.

She looked down between her legs at his amused expression. "It's not funny, Justin."

His lips twitched. "No, indeed it isn't." He spun a "right foot yellow" and easily moved around her, letting her feel his hard cock brush her ass cheek on the way. Linc had his turn, also easily moving into place. His hard cock was now mere inches from her face and she licked her lips, wanting to take it in her mouth and suck on it until he came down her throat.

She spun and almost threw the spinner across the room. It was "right hand red." She'd be sprawled in some weird position she could never hold. She took a deep breath and inched her hand across the bed slowly, her ass lowering slightly. When she was about a millimeter from safety, Justin leaned forward and circled her back hole with his tongue. She cried out at the sensation and went down like a house of cards, her men following her, getting their arms and legs tangled together.

She pushed their heavy appendages off her and sat up giving them the stink eye.

"You cheated. Cheater, cheater, pumpkin eater," she taunted.

Linc rolled over on the bed laughing. "I'm going to be eating something soon, but it won't be pumpkin. It'll be pussy."

She loved seeing him so happy and carefree. She wanted him to be this happy every day. She also desperately wanted him to eat her pussy.

Linc levered up and sat on the edge of the bed, patting his lap. "Over my knees, Leah. You lost. We won. You owe us a spanking."

She wanted this but didn't want to make it too easy. They'd had so many things come to them easily in the last years. She didn't want to be one of them. She stood and crossed her arms over her breasts and scowled at them.

"I want a rematch. A fair one."

Justin lounged against the pillows like a sultan. "Do you think the outcome would be any different if we played fair? It just would have taken longer. The sooner you lose, the sooner we can have some real fun."

Shit, she couldn't argue with his logic. She'd been egging them on about a spanking and bondage for weeks. They'd dragged their heels and talked about building trust before they got kinky. They'd spanked her during sex, of course, but this was different. This was submissive in a way she'd never dreamed, but wanted badly.

Why am I standing here acting like this wasn't my idea?

Linc patted his legs again and she knelt down on the floor and leaned over his muscular thighs, the rough hair erotic against her bare skin. Justin came around to help and lifted her further over until her ass was in the air and her palms were on the floor. She kicked her feet a little but Justin easily caught her ankles and controlled them.

"No kicking, honey. You'll take out an eye. You know what they say. It's all fun and games until someone loses an eye. And 'sorry' doesn't put back an eye."

She could actually hear the smirk in Justin's voice and kicked at him one more time. He chuckled and anchored her legs wide apart, every wet inch of her pussy on display.

Linc's hand rubbed circles on her ass cheeks, warming up the skin. She was already painfully aroused and he'd barely touched her. Just the thought of being spanked had her on the edge of orgasm. She was probably making a puddle on Linc's thighs.

Linc reached between her legs and fondled her clit. "Say you want it, Leah. Ask me to spank you."

The blood was rushing to her head and she braced her palms on the floor. "Please spank me."

For a moment she didn't think he was going to do it, but then his hand came down on her bottom. He didn't spank her very hard, just enough to send heat to her cunt and make her squirm for more. His hand began raining down on her ass, getting harder with every stroke. She was moaning and wriggling, but Justin held her firmly in place. She rubbed her clit against Linc's leg, trying to get herself over as the heat from the spanking sent pleasure to every corner of her body.

Linc paused and played with her pussy, torturing her swollen nub and making her beg for release.

"I need to come! Let me come." Her voice sounded strained and weak.

"Look at the way she's rubbing against me, Justin. Like a cat." Linc smacked her bottom hard. "No coming yet. It will be better if you wait."

She called him a nasty name that only made him laugh. Justin anchored her more firmly in place so she couldn't get any pressure on her clit. Linc resumed spanking her and didn't stop until her bottom was white hot and her pussy was clenching with need.

Linc and Justin helped her to her feet before laying her on the bed. She winced as her sore bottom brushed the sheets. Linc pulled her arms over her head while Justin pulled an ankle wide. They were restraining her to the bed with padded cuffs just like in the book she had given Justin to read. Her arousal hitched up several more notches. She'd read about this but the reality was much more exciting. Before she knew it, she was tied spread-eagle to the bed. She felt a little sorry for the fictitious heroine. She'd been tied to the bed like Leah, but the heroine didn't have Justin and Linc.

Justin perched between her splayed legs and ran a finger down her drenched slit.

"Look how shiny her pussy and thighs are. She's very turned on. I've got to taste her honey."

Yes, yes, yes.

Justin's tongue teased every inch of her cunt, slowly tracing her folds and flitting over her clit. She pulled at the restraints but they wouldn't budge. The feeling of helplessness moved her closer to orgasm and she was teetering on the edge in moments. Linc licked and nipped at her nipples, sending spirals of pleasure to her abdomen. She needed to come and she needed to come now.

She opened her mouth to beg, but screamed instead as Justin's lips closed over her button, scraping the side lightly with his teeth. The restraints added an entirely new dimension to her climax as she shook and trembled with each wave. When she could finally open her eyes and talk, she saw two grinning men looking very satisfied with themselves, as if they'd invented the wheel or discovered fire.

"Stop grinning."

Linc stroked his goatee, his smile turning devilish. "For someone at our mercy, you sure are bossy. Seems to me like you should show some respect. Call me Sir."

She gritted her teeth. She was going to poison Linc's food when he untied her.

"Sir. Please stop grinning, *Sir*."

Justin body shook trying to hold in his laughter. "What about me? I want a title, too. Call me Admiral."

She wanted to kick him in the balls. They both had entirely too much self-esteem. Too many women had pandered to their egos over the years.

"You don't even own a boat. I'll call you Golden Boy. How's that?"

Justin's eyes narrowed and his lips pursed.

Oh shit.

Linc lounged back on the bed. "You've done it now, baby. You've awakened the beast. He hates to be called that, you know."

That was exactly why she'd said it, but now it didn't seem like such a good idea. Justin was fishing around in the nightstand for something and giving her an evil grin. He crowed in triumph and held it up for her inspection.

"What is it?"

Justin chuckled. "Nipple clamps. Give me a hand here, Linc. Miss Bookworm is going to show me some respect."

Within seconds they had each taken a nipple in their mouth and sucked it taut and hard, before attaching the clamps. The metal bit into her nipple and she had to relax and breathe through the pain. Already her pussy was responding by dripping honey on the sheets and down her thighs. They were watching her closely waiting for her to yell or scream for them to be removed. By the time she'd caught her breath to do just that, she didn't want them taken off after all. Although the feeling of constant pressure on her nipples was unusual, it felt good. Very good.

She felt the heat sweep through her body when Linc delved into her pussy.

"She loves it. She's soaking the sheets with her cream. Looks like you're going to have to find another way to make her call you

Admiral."

She moaned as Linc started finger-fucking her, his thumb grazing her clit. Justin sat back with a thoughtful expression.

"I have just the thing for her." He reached into the drawer beside the bed again and Leah shook her head. She couldn't take much more stimulation.

"Admiral. Admiral, okay."

A smile played around Justin's mouth. "Admiral what?"

She sighed. "Stop grinning, Admiral."

He closed the drawer and sat back on his heels with a smile. "Thank you, honey. I like it when you call me Admiral. And by the way, I do own a boat. A yacht. It's docked in Miami. We'll have to take it down to the Keys sometime."

She rolled her eyes. "I should have known. I forget who you are sometimes."

His expression turned soft. "That's what I love about you. You don't give a shit who I am or what I have."

She felt her heart turn over in her chest. "You love me?"

It was his turn to roll his eyes. "Of course. What do you think that song was all about? Friendship and deep respect?"

She felt tears prick the back of her eyes. "I didn't want to assume anything. I love you, too."

Justin pointed to a grinning Linc. "He loves you, too, by the way. You've got us wrapped around your pretty little finger. Luckily, we like it that way."

Linc shrugged. "She already knows I love her."

Leah tried to twist in the restraints to look Linc in the eye. "I didn't! How was I supposed to know you loved me? You never told me."

Linc had the nerve to look outraged. "I told you I couldn't read. I've never told that to a living soul. Of course I love you. You had to know it. I bared my soul to you."

Leah chewed her lip, realizing she should have known it. Linc was a strong man who kept his own counsel. He never would have told her something as deeply personal as that if he hadn't loved her.

"You're right. I should have known. I love you, too. Both of you, so much. But this is wrong. All wrong."

Both men frowned and she laughed. "You're not supposed to tell a woman you love her when she's tied to the bed. It's tacky. You're supposed to tell her with candlelight and champagne."

Linc stroked his chin. "What are we supposed to do when the woman we love is tied to the bed?"

Leah giggled, her heart full of love for these men. "You're supposed to fuck her. I've been waiting patiently."

Linc snorted. "Patient? You're not the most patient of women. But, you are right. We need to fuck you."

Justin moved up to start playing with the clamps on her nipples, sending flames licking along her skin. Linc retrieved a condom from the nightstand and rolled it on before taking his place between her legs. His cock pressed against her wet cunt and he thrust hard, filling her completely and taking her breath away. She loved having her men inside of her, stretching her. Fucking her.

She let her eyelids flutter closed, savoring the sensation of the two of them joined.

"Fuck me."

Chapter Thirteen

Linc fucked her hard and slow, taking his time with each thrust. She was hot and wet and she hugged his aching cock like a glove, squeezing him and making his balls draw up and the pressure in his lower back increase. He wanted to make this last forever.

He motioned to Justin to untie her arms and legs from the bedposts. She immediately wrapped her legs around his waist and scraped her nails down his back. She loved this as much as he did. He loved her honest responses, no artifice or games. She didn't play hard to get or coy. She wanted them as much as they wanted her. Well, almost. At this moment, he wanted Leah more than he wanted anything in his life.

He needed to slow everything down and get control again. He rolled over so she was straddling him on top. She grabbed his shoulders to steady herself. The clamps on her nipples swayed deliciously right above his lips. He latched onto one and gave it a tug, feeling her cunt ripple on his cock.

"She likes the clamps, Justin. We'll have to use them more often."

Justin sat behind her and rubbed her back and shoulders. Leah had her eyes closed and was lost to the passion and pleasure as she moved up and down slowly. Linc nodded to Justin. Time to send her higher.

Justin began to spank her as she rode Linc's cock. Her movements sped up and soon she was slamming down on him over and over, sending lightning shocks to his balls. He couldn't take much more, his jaw tight with the effort to not explode.

Fuck, she looked gorgeous. Her head was thrown back, her long, thick hair in disarray around her face. She had a dreamy smile on her face, her skin glowing with perspiration.

Justin kissed her neck and shoulders and his hands reached around, hesitating for a moment. Linc nodded and Justin pulled first one clamp and then the other off, before reaching down to play with her swollen clit.

Leah screamed as the blood rushed back into her nipples and her climax hit her. Her pussy clamped down on his cock and he couldn't hold back any longer. He arched his back and thrust upward as she came down on his cock. His fingers bit into her hips, and she would probably have bruises tomorrow from where he held her still. He felt his cock jerk, his orgasm shooting out his balls into the condom. It seemed to go on forever, and yet it was over too soon.

He cuddled her close, the perspiration on their bodies cooling quickly. He gently placed her in Justin's arms while he took care of the condom and came back with a warm washcloth to clean her up. She was curled into Justin's chest, a smile playing on her lips.

Justin took the washcloth from Linc and began to run it over her thighs. "I think you wore her out, buddy. She's almost asleep."

Her eyes popped open. "Am not. I'm not tired. I could go all night, if you must know."

Justin laughed. "Good to know. Unfortunately, we can't. Eventually, we'll need to have some recovery time. But if you're not too tired...I haven't come yet."

Linc lounged against the headboard, content to watch his best friend and the woman they loved more than life. This was how it was supposed to be.

Leah was giggling as Justin tickled her, kissing and nibbling at her ribs and belly. Justin swept Leah up in his arms and headed for the bathroom. He looked over his shoulder and smirked.

"Better rest up. Leah's going to wear me out in the shower, and then I'll need a break. She wants to go all night."

Linc chuckled and pulled the covers over him. He already had plans for round two with the woman of his dreams.

* * * *

They loved her. She should have known it before. They'd shown her in so many ways, but she'd been insecure. She knew it now, and she could feel it. It radiated from every pore of her men. She wanted a lifetime with them to show them how much she loved them. She had so much love to give these men.

Justin set her down gently on her feet in the large en suite bathroom. She grabbed some fluffy bathsheets while he turned the shower on, both the tall and the short showerheads, for her. Justin and Linc had made certain she had a complete copy of all her toiletries in this bathroom that she had at home. She'd used their two-in-one shampoo only once and it wasn't something she ever wanted to repeat. Her thick head of hair had been a mess the entire day.

Justin helped her into the shower and pulled her close, pressing her back against the tile wall and kissing her until her head spun. He tasted like coffee and chocolate. He had a sweet tooth and he had a hidden stash in his office that he shared with her and no one else.

She stood on her toes and pressed her lips to the column of his neck, letting the water sluice over both of them, the steam cocooning them in their own private world. She continued her path, kissing and licking all over his chest, drawing groans every time she brushed against his hard and ready cock. He'd already waited for his turn and she wouldn't keep him waiting much longer.

She pressed a kiss to his washboard abs, letting her tongue trace the ridges.

"I love you, Justin. Thank you for being patient with me."

His fingers came up under her chin so she was looking up into his brilliant blue eyes. "Thank you for loving me. Thank you for loving Linc. We're all going to be very happy together. I'm going to make sure of it."

She licked down the center of his flat stomach, going to her knees.

"Me, too. I know just how to make you happy."

He caught her under her arms and pulled her back to her feet. "Uh-uh. I want to come in your pussy. If you put your hot mouth on me, I'm done for."

She trailed her hands down his torso and encircled his cock with her hands.

"That's kind of the point."

He shook his head and poured some shampoo into the palm of his hand. "Not yet. First, let's get squeaky clean. Then, we can have some dirty fun."

She couldn't argue with his plan. His talented fingers were massaging the shampoo into her scalp, sending tingles all the way to her toes. It felt so decadent to have a sexy man washing her hair in a steamy shower. She ducked under the spray to rinse her hair while he soaped his own hair under the taller showerhead. She reached for the shower gel, but he got there first.

"I'll wash you, then you wash me, honey."

She felt her pussy practically liquefy as his hands glided up and down her body. It was hot everywhere he touched and he made sure his fingers brushed her nipples and clit with every stroke. By the time he finished, she was shaking and ready to beg for his cock.

She started by soaping his broad shoulders, letting her palms slide over the firm muscles. His chest was next, down to his stomach, ignoring his straining cock. If she touched it, she wouldn't stop until he was coming. She knelt to soap his thighs, the soap dripping down his long legs. The only thing that was left was his thick cock.

Her fingers traced the roadmap of veins and her other hand gently soaped his balls, already pulled close to his body. He growled, and before she could catch her breath, his lips crushed hers in a searing kiss.

"Fuck me, Justin. I need you."

She thought he was leaving her, but he was only reaching for a condom he'd left on the bathroom vanity. Her fumbling fingers helped him roll it on. She was desperate to feel his cock deep inside her. They hadn't been together long, but she was already addicted to being with her men, loving them.

"Will it always be like this? Will we always feel this unbearable need to be together?"

Justin had much more experience with sex and relationships than she did.

He gave her a lopsided grin. "I think we will. I've never felt like this with anyone in my life. Only you. I know Linc feels the same. I think you're stuck with us chasing you around the bedroom for the rest of your life."

"Sounds good to me. I won't be running very fast."

He lifted her legs and wrapped them around his waist, bracing her against the shower wall. His cock nudged at her entrance and she pressed her hips forward, impaling herself on his dick. They both groaned at the sensation and she buried her face in his neck.

He pulled out slowly, then thrust back in hard, his groin rubbing against her swollen clit. Over and over, faster and faster, he pistoned in and out of her. Her back was pressed against the tile and her hands were anchored to his shoulders. The steam swirled around them as the room tilted and spun.

"Oh god, oh god, oh god. I'm going to come, Justin."

Her voice sounded strange in the confines of the shower, gravelly and needy. He continued fucking her, making sure every stroke rubbed her in just the right spot to send her over. Her toes were curled and she couldn't hold back any longer. She dug her nails into his back and cried out his name.

His fingers tightened on her hips and he thrust one last time as deep as he could go. His breath came out in a hiss and his jaw was clenched. She wanted to watch his expression as he came but she was too overcome with her own climax, the pleasure sweeping through her making her curse and tremble.

He pressed his forehead to hers as their breathing slowed to normal. He carefully set her feet down on the floor of the shower and for a moment she wasn't sure if her knees would hold her. He kept a reassuring arm around her waist until she could stand on her own.

"That was amazing. You're amazing." His breath was close to her ear.

She turned and kissed his jaw. "So are you. I think I need to rest before the next round though."

He turned off the water and helped her out of the shower, wrapping a towel around her.

"Are you really determined to make love all night? Linc and I are lucky men."

She giggled and grabbed his towel, drying his yummy body herself. "If I have my way, you and Linc will be exhausted men. I've only just begun my assault on your bodies."

Justin laughed and spread his arms in surrender. "Assault away, honey. I'm all yours."

She was all theirs, too. These men belonged with her.

* * * *

Justin opened his eyes to sunshine streaming in the windows and Leah's talented tongue licking his cock and balls. Sometime in his sleep, his fingers had already tangled in her hair, and he groaned as she slid her mouth down to the head of his dick, tracing the slit and making him crazy.

"Fuck, what a way to wake up." His voice sounded choked and rough this early in the morning, especially after a show.

He turned to find Linc on the other side of the bed with a smirk and a hard-on.

"She woke me up about ten minutes ago the very same way. I'm not completely sure, but I think she's in the mood to fuck. She got me hard and horny then abandoned me for you."

Leah lifted her head. "I said I was good for all night and I meant it. Are you complaining?"

Justin shook the sleep away. "Hell, no. I just didn't get much sleep last night."

None of them had. He and Linc had taken turns making love to Leah until about two in the morning when they'd all fallen asleep. His sexy woman was feeling frisky again and he was definitely in the mood and rested up to take care of her. In fact, he had an idea he knew would blow her mind. He nodded to Linc to get behind Leah, while Justin pulled her off his cock and up his body.

He sat up and captured a pouting nipple with his teeth, worrying it between his lips and feeling her thighs tighten on his hips. Linc was kissing his way down her delicate spine and she was already squirming in their arms, trying to rub herself against him. He played with her nipples and while Linc nibbled at her neck.

"Honey, we want to fuck you." Justin kissed her lips, letting his tongue play with hers.

"Yes, yes, yes," she breathed.

He and Linc exchanged a glance, their minds completely in tune with each other. Linc bit her earlobe and she moaned.

"We want to fuck you together, baby. Me and Justin at the same time. He'll fuck your pretty pussy, and I'll fuck your tight ass."

Her eyes went wide. "Both of you at the same time?"

Justin thought he saw panic. He and Linc wouldn't scare or hurt their woman for the world. "It's up to you, honey. We don't have to if you don't want to. It's okay if you don't want to."

She shook her head. "I do want to. I'm just a little nervous, that's all. I've heard that it can hurt sometimes."

Linc pulled her back into his arms. "I'll go slow. If you want to stop at any time, we will. We don't want to force you or hurt you. We want you to enjoy this."

She nodded, a smile blooming on her beautiful face. "Let's do this. I want to be with both of you at the same time."

Justin snagged a condom from the bedside table and rolled it on, beckoning to her.

"First, let's get you on top of me, then Linc can work his magic."

She was already wet and he slid inside her easily, her muscles sucking him in and holding him tight. It was going to get even tighter when Linc worked his way into her ass. He gritted his teeth together to hold back as she tightened her pussy on his cock. He smacked her ass, leaving a pink handprint on the creamy skin.

"Behave or this will be over before it starts. No working those tight muscles on my dick." He patted his chest. "Lie down here and stay still. Just relax and let Linc in, okay?"

She giggled, her expression innocent. "I have no idea what you're talking about. I didn't do anything with my pussy."

Linc smacked her other ass cheek, leaving a matching handprint. "No lying, either. Now lie down before I decide spanking you would be more fun."

She pouted but did as she was told. She looked over her shoulder and gave Linc a provocative look. "Don't hold back. I want every inch you've got."

* * * *

Her heart was pounding in her chest but arousal was curling in her belly. She was already stuffed full of one man and she had just taunted the other to give her everything he had. She had to be certifiably insane.

Linc had rolled on a condom and pulled a bottle of lube from the drawer. She shivered as it dripped down her crack.

"Shit, that's cold."

Linc chuckled. "It'll warm up in a minute. Justin, distract our woman for a few minutes."

Justin rolled her nipples, still sensitive from the clamps the night before, between his thumb and fingers. She squirmed on his cock and then froze as she felt Linc's finger press at her back hole. She held her breath as more lube was added and his finger pushed insistently, but gently.

"Breathe, baby. Breathe. Relax and push out for me."

She blew out her breath and relaxed, allowing his finger to breach the tight ring of muscles. He moved his finger in and out before adding a second. She felt more of a stretch, the burn, and then sparkles of pleasure. His rough fingers were rubbing dark and naughty nerves and she moaned when he added a third finger, stretching her wider than she'd ever been.

"Are you okay? Do you need me to stop?"

His voice was full of concern and his fingers stilled. She wriggled her bottom at him, causing Justin to groan at the friction on his cock.

"Don't stop. I need your cock inside me," Leah begged.

"Easy, baby. You'll get it. You'll get everything you ever want with me and Justin."

Right now she only needed her men. She felt the trickle of lube and then the blunt end of his cock pressing at her back entrance. She relaxed, breathing in and out as the pressure built. When the head of his cock was finally inside her, she pushed back to get more of him.

"No, not yet." His hands were firm on her hips, holding her still. "I don't want you to be sore tomorrow. We'll take this slow."

He held her motionless as he pushed forward, then pulled back, again and again, gaining purchase with each gentle thrust. When he finally thrust all the way in, she cried out at the sensation of being completely filled. Justin was playing with her nipples and Linc was kissing her shoulders and neck, praising her and telling her what a good girl she was.

She was burning up, the flames consuming her body, already balancing on the edge of orgasm. She braced her palms on Justin's chest and started moving back and forth in tiny amounts, mere inches, but already sending arrows of delight to her clit. Her men started to pull out and thrust back in, getting into a rhythm quickly. When Justin would withdraw, Linc would thrust back in, rubbing his cock over those sensitive nerves in her backside. When Linc would pull out, Justin would thrust in hard, gliding over her G-spot and grinding against her clit. Every stroke sent her closer and closer to release.

She was packed so full of cock it was as if she could feel every ridge and vein on their thick shafts. Her world narrowed to just the three of them, the press of flesh on flesh, the smell of sex, their gasps of pleasure, and the taste of salt on their skin. She was beyond words, beyond thought. She was a mass of sensation and pleasure, going toward something shimmering in the distance, but slightly out of reach.

Linc reached around her and pressed on her clit and she was suddenly there. She screamed as she reached the pinnacle, her body slamming back into Linc's. He held her while the waves shook her, almost painful in their intensity. As she started to come down, Justin thrust in one last time. She felt his cock swell and saw his face contort with passion. He was breathing hard and he sat up and captured her lips in a savage kiss that left her dizzy and panting.

As Justin collapsed back on the bed, Linc sped up his thrusts, finally groaning his release. His hands cupped her breasts and his teeth bit into the softness of her shoulder. The edge of pain sent her over again and she shook with a miniorgasm that surprised her. She'd never come without clit stimulation before, but then she'd never been made love to like her men were loving her this morning.

And it was love. This wasn't just sex. This was full-on, heart-dropping, stomach-churning love. The kind of love anyone would be lucky to get.

The men held her close, their legs twined together. Finally, Linc started to pull out very slowly, her muscles protesting.

"Easy, baby. I need to take care of the condom. Justin, too."

She felt bereft as Linc disappeared into the bathroom. He was back in seconds and held her while Justin did the same. She was planning on falling back asleep when Linc tugged her out of bed and scooped her into his arms, heading for the bathroom.

"Let's shower and hit the diner for breakfast. I want to show you off to the entire town."

She giggled. "Maybe I want to show you both off, too. I could make you wear T-shirts that say 'Leah's hot studs' on the front. What do you think?"

Linc waggled his eyebrows as Justin turned on the shower. "I think we need to get some shirts made up. We'll get one made for you also."

"What will mine say?"

Linc smiled. "Our dream come true."

Leah sniffled as he set her feet down in the shower. Her boys could be sweet and romantic when they wanted to be. They were her dream come true. She's always believed in fairy tales, and now she was living one.

Chapter Fourteen

"I'm happy, okay? We're really happy." Leah laughed and bit into the succulent pot roast. She was attending the Monday night dinner at the diner with Jillian, Cassie, Becca, and Ava. She'd been so busy with Justin and Linc she hadn't been in a few weeks and the women were bursting with questions.

"Damn, this pot roast is delicious," Leah raved. "I've got to learn to cook this. Justin and Linc would love it."

"Thinking homey, domestic thoughts, are we?" Cassie teased. "Next stop is marriage-city."

The other women laughed and nodded, but Leah rolled her eyes. "I'm not sure my men are marriage-minded. I know they love me and I know they're committed to me, but we've never talked the Big 'M.'"

Ava nodded. "It's a big step. My boys knew I had trust issues, so they waited a little while. By the time they proposed, I was at 'hell yeah.' I can't wait to be their wife."

Jillian dug into her chicken-fried steak with relish. "How are the wedding plans coming? Are you still planning an autumn wedding?"

"Yes, we are. The wedding colors will be an autumn palette. Think big, huge bouquets of flowers with a riot of colors, a tiered wedding cake in chocolate and gold. We want a sit-down dinner but a dessert buffet afterward."

"Fireworks, too?" Becca laughed. "It must be nice planning a wedding with no budget."

Ava blushed. "My men are good to me. I would have been happy with a small wedding, but you know how they are. You can take the boys out of New York, but you can't take the New York out of the boys. They said they're only getting married once and want to do it big. I had to talk them out of horse-drawn carriages."

Leah wrinkled her nose. "Horses can do smelly things."

Ava nodded vigorously. "Agreed. I put my foot down on that one."

Leah turned to Becca. "By the way, thanks for meeting with Logan and Meyer. I know they probably asked some personal questions and you were awesome to talk to them."

Becca waved away her concern. "They seem like really nice guys. We liked them a lot. They did ask some personal questions, but were careful to stay on the safe side of the boundary. Mostly they were concerned with the logistics of making this work. I got the impression the sexual side was taken care of. They admitted they'd had sex together with a woman, but hadn't found one they wanted to make a commitment to. I know Mark and Travis had a great deal to say on that subject. You know, waiting until you find the right one, making her the center of the relationship." Becca leaned forward. "We should find a woman to fix them up with."

Jillian's expression was surprised. "Are they moving here? I thought they lived in Los Angeles."

Becca grinned. "They do, but we put the full-court press on them to think about moving here. They've fallen in love with the town but aren't sure about their business. If we could just find a woman for them to fall for it would be a done deal."

Cassie sat back replete. "What exactly is their business again? It's some kind of security, right?"

Leah shrugged. "Best as I can tell, they do security checks, you know, background information. I guess rich and famous people like to know personal details about the people they work with and spend time with. I think they also set up security systems and such. We didn't talk about it in detail."

"Is that what they're doing for Linc and Justin?" Ava asked.

"I think so."

Jillian pushed her food around on her plate. "That doesn't concern you a little? Don't you wonder who they're having checked out?"

Leah raised an eyebrow. "I know who they're having checked out and I'm not worried. They don't seem to have a care in the world, so I'm not concerned in the least."

Cassie sipped her iced tea. "You're so serene all the time. I'd be driving Zach and Chase crazy with questions."

Leah shook her head. "I'm not worried at all. If anything was going on, Linc and Justin would, for sure, tell me."

* * * *

Linc's phone starting ringing just as he and Justin entered their office at the club. They were planning to head home soon to meet Leah after her Monday night dinner with the girls.

Linc groaned when he saw the caller. "I'm putting this call on speaker. It's Bobbi."

He accepted the call and sat down at his desk. "Hey, Bobbi. What's going on?"

Justin perched on the edge of the desk with a wary expression. They both wondered what Bobbi thought she had on Justin.

"Linc, what a pleasure to talk to you. I'm calling you about the concert tour. Have you had a chance to reconsider the offer?"

"I haven't changed my mind," Justin answered. "I'm opting out. Good luck, though. Sounds like it should be a big one."

There was a long silence. Justin and Linc exchanged a glance while they waited for Bobbi's reply. Hopefully, she would tip her hand.

"I'm sorry you feel that way, Justin. We've been friends for a long time."

Linc shook his head. They'd never been friends. Not really.

"I hate to do this, but I need you on this tour. I need you to say yes."

"I won't say yes." Justin pulled up a chair from his desk and relaxed back in it with a grin. After several discussions with Justin, Linc knew there was nothing Bobbi could say that would compel Justin to do the tour.

"I think you will." There was anger in Bobbi's voice now. She was clearly not happy with them. "I don't think you want your devoted fans to know what you've been up to. I'd hate to have to tell them."

Justin leaned toward the phone. "Why don't you tell me what I've been up to that anyone would give a shit about?"

Bobbi laughed but she sounded more triumphant than happy. "Threesomes. You and Linc like it kinky. I have three women who are willing to make a statement to the press that you had sex with them together. They're also willing to testify you're a little perverted, liking spankings and double-penetration sex. You even moved to a kinky town and are double-teaming your little girlfriend. What would the world think about their Golden Boy if they found out?"

Linc shook his head in amazement. They'd never flaunted their sexual proclivities but they hadn't buried them either. The fact was they never thought anyone gave a damn about what they did in the privacy of their bedroom as long as Justin churned out the hits.

Justin propped his feet up on the desk. "Go ahead."

Crickets could have been heard in the background. "What do you mean?" Bobbi's voice had lost its bravado. She sounded unsure of herself now.

"I mean, go ahead. Tell anyone you want. We don't give a damn."

"You'll lose everything. You'll lose your fans and your career."

"I won't lose anything I value. I left my career behind, and if my fans don't approve, well, that's their business. I won't let you blackmail me, Bobbi."

"I'll call a press conference today. I'll tell them everything." Her voice was shaky.

Linc snorted. "Tell them. They'll talk about us for a few days, then somebody else will fuck up and we'll be old news. But, if I were you I'd be careful, Bobbi."

"Why should I be careful?" Bobbi sounded like she was crying now. Linc hated being a hard-ass, but he didn't tolerate people threatening them.

"I doubt you want people talking about you. You've got a few skeletons, too."

Logan and Meyer had called him last night and filled them in on Bobbi's checkered past. They didn't want to use any of it against her in the press, but Linc wouldn't hesitate to point out she had something to lose herself if she persisted with this.

"I hate you," Bobbi spat. "I hate both of you."

"We can live with it," Linc answered. "I'm sorry you're in the mess you're in, but you can't go around blackmailing people into doing whatever you want. Life doesn't work that way."

"You'll be sorry. Both of you will."

Justin shook his head sadly. "The only thing we're sorry for is ever doing business with you in the first place. Take some advice, Bobbi. Straighten up and do things by the book. Treat people decently. In the end, people are all you have, not money, cars, and big houses."

"Fuck you. Fuck both of you. I'm going to get back on top, and when I do I'm going to make sure you never work again." Bobbi hung up.

Linc sighed in relief. "Now we know what she thought she had. She still can't seem to understand we don't want what we had. We want something completely different."

Justin stood up and stared out over the club. "Bobbi's going to have to learn this lesson the hard way." He turned back. "She's mad enough to go to the press. You're the boss. What do you suggest?"

Linc grinned. "I'm going to call Logan and Meyer first and thank them for their help and then get a press conference of our own scheduled. Let's get the truth out there before anyone else. I don't want this to keep haunting us in the future. If we really don't care what people say, let's do it."

Justin nodded. "The truth will set us free. Make your calls."

* * * *

Leah hummed as she climbed the stairs to the office above the club. She'd had a great dinner with the girls and hadn't felt strange or awkward once. She giggled. She was becoming downright extroverted on occasion. Rare occasions, of course.

She pushed open the door to the office and heard Linc and Justin talking along with another voice. She hesitated to interrupt them when they were doing business so she decided to wait until they were done.

"Bobbi's big news was she's planning to tell the world Linc and I share women," Justin could be heard saying. "She knows about Leah, and the town of Plenty. Of course, she says it will ruin my career. I'll lose fans and our lives won't be worth living. She was pretty venal when she called."

"What did you tell her?" She recognized Logan's voice although it was a little distorted. They must be talking on the phone.

Linc pushed back his chair. "What do you think we told her? This isn't going to end well. You know that."

Leah stepped back, almost stumbling on the stairs. She backed down them quickly, her heart breaking into pieces. Someone was going to out Justin and Linc about their relationship with her. Justin would lose many of his fans, possibly friends and family, to make matters worse. It was hard for people outside of a town like this to truly understand ménage. Even Linc had said it wouldn't end well. If the press got a hold of this, it would ruin Justin's legacy. People wouldn't talk about his music anymore. They'd talk about his personal life.

She practically ran down to her car and started driving, not sure where she was going, but knowing she had to put some distance between herself and her men. By the time she reached Main Street, the tears in her eyes had dried. She swallowed the lump in her throat, heartsick at the turn of events. She knew what she had to do. She had to back away from her beloved men. It was the only way to make this situation right. She couldn't let them lose everything they'd worked for because of her.

I love them too much to let them be hurt.

Man, love was painful. Even when Jenny had set her bookstore on fire, her chest hadn't hurt this badly. The only solace she felt was the fact she knew they loved her in return. It wouldn't be easy for any of them, but it had to be done. They were probably trying to work out a gentle way to let her down easy right now.

She found herself at the far end of Main Street, past the historic district, where her father's old mechanic's garage was located. Gabe's motorcycle was parked outside alongside Jason's truck. She didn't know what they were doing there, but she suddenly needed the comfort of family. She wasn't going to be able to get through this broken heart alone.

The front door was locked, but the back door was open, letting in an early spring breeze. She stepped in—the overhead lights up on the high ceiling were lit up—and looked around in confusion. All the car lifts and tools were gone. The space was wide open, with only some sawhorses and tables in the middle of the room. On the tables were hammers, saws, and nails, while in the corner of the large warehouse-like space was a large stack of wood. She spied Gabe and Jason leaning against a counter and talking. It was good to see them so comfortable with each other.

"Hey, what are you guys doing in here?"

Both men started when they saw her, obviously not expecting any company. Gabe straightened up, his shoulders tense.

"Sis, I could ask the same question. What are you doing here? I thought you had a date with Justin and Linc tonight?"

She felt her lips start to tremble and her eyes start to fill with tears. She hated being a crybaby, but she was still reeling from the conversation she'd overheard. Gabe pulled her in for a hug before she could answer.

"Aw, sis. What happened? Do I need to go kick Justin and Linc's asses? Because I will, you know. Jason will, too."

Jason nodded grimly. "They make you cry, I make them cry. Fair is fair."

She shook her head and pulled away, wiping tears from her eyes. "No, it's not their fault."

Gabe crossed his arms over his chest, his eyes narrowed. He was every inch the big brother at this moment. "Then whose fault is it?"

Gabe offered her his bottle of water and she drank gratefully, sinking into the metal folding chair by the counter. "I'm going to end it with them. I have to."

Jason pulled up another chair. "Okay, slow down, think this through, and tell us why you have to end it."

Leah took a deep breath and told them about the phone call she'd overheard. Jason pursed his lips, looking thoughtful. "Leah, you didn't hear the entire conversation. You could have misunderstood something. Did they say they needed to end the relationship?"

She shook her head, sniffling. Gabe handed her a handkerchief. "No, but they said she could make their life not worth living. I don't want their life not worth living. It would be mean to stay with them if this could happen."

Gabe scowled. "They're fucking famous, at least Justin is. They must have thought this whole lifestyle thing through before they came here."

Jason patted her hand. "Something isn't right here. You need to talk to them, honest and open. If you can't be together, you deserve to know the truth and why. Maybe they just need to keep it a secret. Make out like you're only with Linc or something."

That sounded even worse. Pretending not to love one of her men would be impossible. She knew it was written on her face every time she looked at them.

"I can't talk to them. I'll just start crying, and you know men hate a woman crying."

"Can't argue with that," Gabe said. "Why don't you head home and get some sleep. Everything will look better tomorrow."

Leah pushed her glasses up her nose. "I can't go home. They've already left me several messages and the next place they're going to go is my house. I'm not ready to face them."

Jason squeezed her hands. "You have to face them, cuz. You can't avoid this. It's not a book where you don't have to turn the page. This is real life."

Real life sucks. Give me a book any day.

Her head fell back and she slumped in the chair. "I know you're right. I just don't want you to be right."

Gabe laughed. "Sorry, sis. We men are right every now and then. Do you want us to come with you?"

She shook her head and stood up. "No, I'm a grown woman. I can do this." She took a good look around for the first time since arriving. "You never answered me. What are you guys doing here? Not that I'm complaining. It's good to see you two work together again."

Gabe rubbed his chin. "Let's just say Jason got even with me. He's agreed to help me with my project when he has time off."

She raised her eyebrows. "What project is that? It's obvious you're not opening this back up to work on cars. What is this going to be when it grows up? Does the town council know about this?"

The town council was very protective of Plenty and what businesses could open there.

"Yes, I already talked to Zach and Chase about this. I have a permit and everything, little sister. Worried Jason might have to arrest me?"

Gabe was smiling and she felt herself start to smile back. It was hard to be unhappy when her brother was so clearly happy again.

She'd waited a long time to see him this way.

She pointed to Jason. "He'd probably be happy to if it came to that." She walked to the tables in the middle of the room. She didn't know much about carpentry but her brother and cousin were clearly building some kind of furniture. "Are you building furniture? Are you going to sell it?"

Gabe and Jason looked at each other before Gabe answered. "We are building furniture. Bondage furniture."

He paused and waited for her reaction. The problem was she wasn't sure what her reaction was going to be. She'd thought her brother said "bondage furniture."

"Um, can you say that again?"

Gabe ran his hands over a piece that was in the process of being assembled. "Bondage furniture. I'm opening a BDSM club here in Plenty. When I was away, I worked as a Dom in a couple of clubs. It was a way to work on my control and anger issues. It worked and now I'm home."

She turned to Jason. "Are you a Dom, too?"

Jason chuckled, his face pink. "Only a wannabe. Gabe here is the real thing. You should be proud of him, Leah. He worked on his problems and found a way to solve them."

She blinked a few times. "You couldn't try psychotherapy?"

Gabe nodded. "I did try that. That's where I found out about BDSM. It was just the thing I needed. It saved me really."

She pressed a hand to her forehead. "I can't think about this right now. I have to deal with Justin and Linc first. Then I'll deal with my brother the Dom." She picked up her purse and headed for the door. She turned back one more time. "What makes you think anyone in Plenty will come to a sex club anyway?"

Gabe frowned. "It's not a sex club, it's a BDSM club. And are you kidding? All the alpha males in this town? This is like shooting fish in a barrel. I can show them how to give their women pleasure like they've never known, but keep it safe, sane, and consensual."

She rubbed her temples. She didn't want to hear about her brother's sex life.

"What are you going to name it?"

Jason laughed. "I suggested Plenty of Discipline." He pointed to Gabe. "He had other ideas."

Gabe looked around with pride. "I'm calling it Original Sin."

"Oh, good name." She headed for the door, slightly light-headed. This had been the strangest evening and was only going to get worse. Much worse.

Chapter Fifteen

Leah was halfway home when she pulled over to the side of the road. She didn't like herself very much at the moment. She'd worked hard to put her wallflower, bookworm past behind her. She'd vowed she wouldn't fade into the background any longer, watching life happen around her. Now here she was, running home to hide, scared to deal with reality.

She reached for the ignition and started the car, turning around and heading back to the club. She wasn't going to fade away any longer. She was going to fight for her happiness.

It was late by the time she pulled into the driveway of their home. She'd already stopped by the club and Cheryl had sent her here. She pushed open the car door just as the garage door lifted and Justin's SUV started backing out. She knew they had spotted her when the truck came to a halt and both Justin and Linc came out of the car with thunderous expressions. They were not happy at all.

Linc had a cell phone pressed to his ear. "She's here now, Gabe. We'll take it from here."

Justin scowled, his brow furrowed. "Where in the hell have you been? We've been calling all over looking for you. You were supposed to meet us at the club a couple of hours ago. We were worried sick."

Her heart started beating fast. She needed to compose herself. "I did come to the club. I heard you on the phone and needed some time to think. I'm here now so we can talk."

The men exchanged a look she couldn't decipher. Had they been planning to tell her about it or keep it a secret?

Linc captured her hand and tugged her into the house. "Let's talk inside. I think we could all use a drink."

She wouldn't argue with that. This evening had been emotionally draining. Linc poured them all a glass of wine while she settled herself on the couch. The men sat on either side of her, boxing her in. Justin set his wine glass on the table, his expression grim.

"I'm not sure I want to know what you needed to think about. Are you rethinking the three of us being together?"

She shook her head. It was time for courage. She chose her words carefully. "No, I wasn't. But I thought you were. I overheard you on the phone saying that if your fans found out about the three of us, it would ruin your career. That your lives wouldn't be worth living and it wouldn't end well."

Linc stood up and started pacing, his expression forbidding. "So you ran away?"

She pushed her hair back from her face. "Yes, and I'm not very proud of my behavior. I should have stayed so we could talk about it, but old habits die hard. I went off by myself. I shouldn't have and I'm sorry."

Justin's expression wasn't any happier. "You didn't believe in us. You didn't trust us."

She nodded, her eyes down. She was ashamed of how she'd acted. These were good men and she should have given them a chance to explain. "I'm sorry. I had a few moments of doubt, but I turned the car around and came here. I do believe in you guys. I swear it."

She took a fortifying sip of her wine. Linc's gaze was focused on her, not leaving her for a second.

"I can see you are sorry," Linc finally said. "I guess we're even. I didn't believe in you and you didn't believe in me. Can we put a stop to this now? We're only making this harder than it needs to be."

Justin fell back against the cushions of the couch. "If you'd just come into the office, we would have explained everything. It's no big deal, honey."

Those words surprised her. "No big deal? Your career could be over and it's no big deal? I don't want to be the reason your fans desert you. You'll come to hate me eventually, resent me."

A smile started stretching across Justin's face. "Honey, I could never hate you. I love you. You do, however, drive me crazy on occasion. This is one of them. You should have stuck around for the entire conversation. All of it. Then you would understand."

"What would I understand?"

Linc perched on the arm of a chair. "Yes, someone was threatening us. Bobbi, the concert promoter we told you about, as you know, she wanted Justin to do a concert tour."

Leah's heart went into her throat. "You're going to do the tour?"

"No, I am not. That's why Bobbi was threatening to expose our relationship. She thought it would compel me to do the tour." Justin laughed as if he didn't have a care in the world, not like someone who had been recently blackmailed. "It didn't. I don't care about my career anymore. I've left it behind. I don't care what people think about us. They can talk and judge all they want. That's why we moved here. To live a quiet life exactly as we want to, on our terms."

"What if the press finds out? Won't they write about us?"

Linc nodded. "Probably. People will act all shocked and outraged, while others will just say it's because Justin's a rock star. Eventually, some other celebrity will do something worse, like get arrested, and people will forget about us. Especially if we do nothing to stay in the spotlight." Linc frowned. "Are you concerned about the press bothering you? We'll make sure you have protection, baby. No one is going to bother you. We already have our publicity people on this, working to control the story if it comes out."

"I'm not worried. Well, I shouldn't say it that way. I'm not worried about what they'll write about me. I have nothing to hide. I'm more worried about what they might write about the entire town. When you live here, you kind of forget we live an unusual lifestyle."

Justin placed his hand over hers, tangling their fingers together.

"We don't think Bobbi will actually go to the press. Logan and Meyer found out a few things she doesn't want revealed. If she goes to the press, she'll be under scrutiny as well. Her credibility will be in question and she's not in a position right now to want anyone looking into her personal life."

"So our relationship will stay a secret?"

Linc sat down next to her, his hard thigh pressed close to hers. "No, we've decided, with your permission of course, to go public with it. This way no one can ever threaten us again. It's better to reveal it ourselves so we have control over the story."

"If I say no?" She looked back and forth between them.

Justin squeezed her hand. "Then we don't say anything. We'll move on and act like this never happened. End of story."

They believed telling the story was the right thing to do. She took a leap of faith and decided to believe in them.

"Do it. Tell them about us. You're right, let's get it out in the open and then we can move on."

Both men smiled, their relief clearly written on their faces. Linc pulled her to her feet, his smile morphing into a devilish grin. "You had us worried sick earlier, baby. Jillian told us you left the diner headed for the club but you never showed. I think you need to be spanked for putting us through that, don't you?"

Her body responded immediately. Honey dripped from her pussy and her nipples hardened, rubbing against the lace of her bra.

She tried to look chastened. "I am sorry. You're right, I do need to be punished."

Justin crowded her back, pressing his hot body against hers. "I think we know how to take care of our woman. Let's head to the bedroom."

* * * *

Linc's cock was pressing against his zipper and demanding

attention. If the entire evening hadn't gone awry at Bobbi's phone call, he would have been balls-deep inside Leah at least once already tonight. He couldn't be too upset at the turn of events, however. She finally seemed to believe in them and their love.

He plucked open the buttons on her silky white blouse while Justin went to work on the zipper of her pants. Within seconds, she was naked, her creamy skin beckoning to his greedy fingers. He couldn't get enough of touching and stroking her soft skin, loving the way it felt under his hands. He buried his face in her neck, breathing in her scent, a mixture of flowers and rain.

They both pressed her back on the bed, wanting to make her crazy with wanting them before warming her ass up for making them worry. He and Justin had been frantic when she hadn't shown up at the club. They'd called her cell phone, her home, the bookstore, and some of her girlfriends she was supposed to have dinner with. Jillian Parks had told them Leah had left the diner heading for the club quite a while before. The thought that something had happened to her on the way, perhaps some kind of an accident, had made his stomach twist into a knot.

Plenty was a safe town, but he'd been reared in the city. He hadn't been able to shake the feeling of foreboding until Gabe had called. Her brother had been closemouthed about why Leah was upset, but had let them know she was on her way back to her home. Luckily, Leah had changed her mind and headed their way. Linc had felt relief like he'd never known when he'd seen her in their driveway.

Her fingers were starting to make their own sensual foray over his skin. She had a hand on each of their arms, rubbing and stroking, sending arrows of pleasure straight to his balls. He wasn't going to last long the way things were going. He needed to slow things down.

"Easy, baby. We've got all night."

She answered his statement by pressing her lips to his, her tongue boldly invading his mouth. He was breathing heavy when they finally broke the kiss, her mouth seeking out Justin's next. Her skin was pink with arousal, her thighs already shiny with her honey. She was the most beautiful woman in the world.

Justin finally ended the kiss and stretched her out on the bed, holding her arms above her head. He gave her a mock scowl.

"Punishment starts now. We're going to keep you on the edge of coming for quite a while. You'll be begging us soon."

She arched her back and pressed out her breasts for their inspection and delight.

"I could start begging right now and save us some time."

Linc laughed. His woman was a pistol. "You can't beg to avoid your punishment. We're going to torture and spank you. Then, you'll beg for real."

She fluttered her lashes. "I'm really sorry for worrying you."

Linc bent over her prone form. "Too late. Besides, you know you want this."

* * * *

She wanted this. Her pussy was clenching and dripping honey on the sheets in response to their dominant tones and actions. She loved feeling helpless with Justin holding her arms down. She wasn't, however, going to make it easy for them. She remembered what the girls had told her. Men liked to win things. They liked to strive.

She sniffed with disdain. "Go ahead. You'll never get me to beg. I dare you to try."

Their eyes immediately lit up with the challenge. She had certainly stoked the fires of their competitiveness and although she might end up begging she would definitely be the winner in the end. They would go all out to make sure they gave her more pleasure than she could handle.

Linc drew circles around her clit very slowly, drawing a shaky moan from her lips. It felt so good, and yes, it was torture as well. It was also totally worth it. Justin leaned forward and used his lips and tongue on her nipples, making them hard and tight. She squirmed in their arms, but Justin held her down easily. She cried out at the sensation when Linc swiped his tongue over her clit.

She wanted to beg him to do it again, but pressed her lips together, determined they would win her submission tonight. She was happy to let them be dominant in the bedroom, but she wanted them to earn the position.

She hissed when Linc pressed a finger deep into her pussy. She could feel the walls of her cunt tighten of their own accord, wanting something to fill it. Justin's teeth gently scraped the sides of her tight nipples and she whimpered, moving closer to the edge of orgasm. Linc pressed a kiss to her inner thigh, trailing kisses down to her pussy, but not placing his mouth where she needed it most.

"Do you need to come, baby?" Linc asked, his tongue teasing the sensitive skin where her thigh met her cunt. "Are you ready to beg?"

She knew she would pay dearly for poking the bear, but it was such fun. She raised her head as far as she could, giving both of them glares.

"Fuck you. You can't make me beg."

She almost laughed at their look of astonishment and then they both grinned, seeing right through her ruse. Justin shook his head and laughed. "Honey, that was a very foolish thing to do. You're going to be waiting twice as long for your orgasm now."

Before she knew it she was turned over on her stomach and Justin's hand came down on her ass cheek, sending heat straight to her already drenched pussy. His left hand still held her hands down while his right spanked her ass hot and hard. Linc's hands were holding her thighs wide apart, her arousal on display. She wasn't fooling anyone with her act of bravado.

The spanking stopped abruptly and Justin's fingers started playing in her cunt, teasing her clit and fucking her pussy. When she was on the verge of coming, his motions would halt, letting her come down slightly, only to start the spanking all over again. He gave her a few more spanks, then started using his fingers in her slit again until she was almost over the edge.

She howled in frustration when he pulled his hand away. "Ready to beg? I can spank and play with your pussy all night."

She shook her head, not trusting her voice. She wanted to beg more than anything at the moment. She needed to come badly, but her men had shown her holding back made the final climax all the more sweet. She would hold out as long as she could.

Justin sighed. "Your decision."

The spanking started again, then the fingers, then the spanking again. It all became of blur of pleasure and heat. She lost track of the time, barely able to remember her own name. Her world was the arousal spiraling through her body, their hands, their mouths and tongues. They used everything they had to lead her to the edge of the precipice without allowing her to go over. The pleasure was so strong it was almost pain.

They'd earned her submission. She swallowed, her mouth dry, and her tongue not working well. She opened her mouth to beg but instead felt her legs being spread wider and her cunt lifted. In the next moment, she felt Linc's mouth on her clit and Justin's voice whispering in her ear.

"Well played, honey. We give in first. Time to come."

It was like a hurricane, taking her breath away and twisting her insides into a knot before it sprang free, sending her higher and higher until she thought she was flying. It shook every inch of her body and she screamed as the pleasure hit a crescendo. They held her until she came back to earth. She should have felt sated and limp, but their hard bodies felt delicious next to hers. All she felt was hungry for more. She needed her men inside of her.

She breathed deeply and smiled. "That was awesome. Amazing."

Linc nibbled on her hip bone. "It looked like fun, baby. You're a tough nut to crack, that's for damn sure."

They didn't need to know how close she was to giving in. She was okay with them being dominant in the bedroom, but not insufferable. Her men had healthy enough egos as it was.

Justin retrieved a condom from the nightstand and rolled it on. She opened her arms to welcome him as Linc kissed his way up to her breasts, taking a nipple in his mouth and sending sparks of pleasure through her body. She felt her body climbing toward orgasm again.

Justin entered her in one hard stroke while Linc played with her nipples and kissed her shoulders. Her hands were free and she grasped Justin's shoulders, her fingers digging into the hard muscles.

"Fuck me. I need you so bad."

He gave her all he had, fucking her hard and fast. Each stroke sent her closer to release, his groin rubbing her clit and his cock stroking her sweet spot. She threw her legs around his waist, loving the hard pounding he was giving her. She raked her nails down his back, urging him to fuck her harder and faster.

Linc reached between them and rubbed her clit, sparking her orgasm. Her pussy clamped down on Justin's cock and he thrust in one last time before stilling inside of her. His eyes were glassy with ecstasy and his face was contorted with passion. He leaned down to kiss her, soft and sweet, before pulling from her still-quivering flesh. He fell to his back and gasped for air.

Then Linc was there. Leaning over her with his devilish smile.

"Are you ready for me, baby? Is it okay?"

She tugged him closer. "It's more than okay. I need you, too."

He entered her slowly, watching her expression and looking into her eyes the entire time. When he was in to the hilt, she sighed at the feeling of being so full, so part of her man. She reached and ran her hands through his silky hair.

"Don't keep me waiting."

He started slowly, letting his cock run over all the sensitive spots in her cunt. She tried to urge him on, but Linc wouldn't be rushed. His thrusts were slow and controlled, his expression stamped with arousal. He was determined to savor every moment of this.

She closed her eyes and let her senses take over. She could smell the scent of sex heavy in the air, mixed with the masculine scents of her men. She could hear their breathing, the moans and the whispers in her ear, promising anything and everything. She could feel their hot skin next to hears, the sheen of sweat, the crinkle of the hair on their arms and legs. Her fingers flexed around Linc's hard biceps, then ran up his shoulders and down his back. She loved the curves and dips of their bodies, so different from her own.

In and out, Linc fucked her, harder and faster with every stroke. She knew he was holding on by a thread. She raised her hips and ground against him, her clit already sensitive and swollen. Justin sucked a nipple into his mouth, biting down until the edge of pain triggered her orgasm. She cried out, bucking underneath Linc. He slammed home, his teeth clenched, and his jaw tight. Her pussy was so sensitive she could feel every jerk of his cock as he came hard inside the condom.

He collapsed, carefully rolling to her side so as not to squash her. The men disappeared for a few minutes to take care of the condoms, before rejoining her in bed. They lay together quietly, touching and stroking, letting time gently tick away. It was Justin who finally spoke.

"Don't ever think about leaving us, Leah. You're everything to us. If you run, we'll just come find you."

Linc captured her chin and turned her so she could look into his deep brown eyes.

"We love you. We'll always put you first."

She was overwhelmed and humbled. She could feel the love radiating from them. They'd left her in no doubt.

"I'll never run again. If we have an issue, we'll face it. Together."

Nothing felt as good as together did with these men.

Chapter Sixteen

Leah stepped back from the book display with a sigh of satisfaction. It had taken some time to get it just right, but she was happy with the results. The new releases could easily be seen by anyone walking down the street window-shopping, but were also easily accessible to shoppers browsing in the store.

The bell over the door chimed and she turned to see her two handsome men stride into the store. Her heart lurched in her chest and her knees turned to jelly. She wondered if she'd ever get used to seeing them. They were so sexy and their smiles alone could send her arousal into orbit. She rushed over to give them welcoming kisses. She'd gotten over her initial shyness, now proud to call these men her own.

They kissed her back with enthusiasm, Justin at her front and Linc at her back. This was her favorite place to be, sandwiched between her two men. She giggled as Linc's lips nipped at her neck.

"Behave yourself, Linc Davis. This is my place of business."

She tried to sound stern, but it came out breathless instead. These men were a lethal combination.

"We came to kidnap you, baby," Linc chuckled. "We're taking you away from here."

Leah glanced at the clock. It was barely half past ten. "It's too early for lunch, guys. Besides, Alyssa doesn't get here until one."

Alyssa was her new hire so Leah could spend more time with Justin and Linc. She'd only been there a few weeks, but already was proving to be a godsend.

Justin looked over his shoulder. "We've got that taken care of.

Gabe is going to watch the store."

Her brother was entering the store with a mischievous grin. Luckily, he wasn't wearing his usual uniform of tattered blue jeans and a sweaty T-shirt. He'd been working on his new BDSM club night and day for weeks now and he'd seemed to be perpetually grimy and tired. He looked clean, if not refreshed, today in a pair of khaki dress pants and a button-down shirt, rolled up at the sleeves.

"You're going to watch the store for me? Since when are you interested in the bookstore?"

Even as kids, Gabe had been more interested in being outside than in the store, reading a book.

Gabe quirked an eyebrow. "I'm a voracious reader, I'll have you know. I think I can handle ringing up sales for the good people of Plenty. Alyssa can help me if I have a question."

"Alyssa won't be here until one. Lunch won't take that long."

All three men gave each other a look that made her instantly start to worry. She'd realized having two men meant they often conspired together, and today seemed to be one of those days. She could handle her men, but she needed to know what they were up to this time.

"I know that look, so spill it. One of you better start talking."

She looked from one to the other, knowing Justin would be the first to break. When he did, she had to hide her smile.

"It's not just lunch, honey. We'll be gone a little longer than that."

She crossed her arms over her chest and gave them a suspicious look. "Why? What are we doing?"

Linc winked at her and hustled her out the front door, ignoring her protests.

"You need to stop worrying and trust us, baby. You're going to love this, we promise."

Before she knew it she was sitting in the back of Justin's SUV heading toward Orlando. Every time she tried to question them about what they were up to, they dodged the question and changed the subject. Finally, they pulled up in front of a large, fancy hotel.

Several people came out to meet them, ushering them into a long corridor in the back of the hotel. One of the men nodded to Justin and Linc. "They're ready for you. Are you ready for them?"

Both her men nodded and turned to her. "Wait here for us. We need to take care of this one thing, then we're all yours."

Justin and Linc went through a doorway and Leah was able to see the room was full of people and cameras. A table was placed at the front of the room and Justin and Linc sat down, looking happy and relaxed. Linc raised his hand and the room went silent.

"I'll read from a prepared statement, then we'll take a few questions."

It's a press conference.

She'd seen a few on television, but never in person. Linc was reading a statement about their relationship and explaining polyamory. He concluded by saying they wanted to live their life quietly and away from the public, and wouldn't allow disapproval by others to dictate how they lived their life.

The questions came fast and furious. The reporters wanted to know her name, which Linc quickly deflected, telling them they were public figures but Leah was not. She wouldn't be subject to their probing and prying. She felt a hand on her shoulder and turned to see Sheriff Ryan Parks.

He was the last person she had expected to see. "What are you doing here?"

Ryan waggled his eyebrows. "I'm here to scare them. Watch me."

He walked into the press conference and stepped up to the microphone. He was a tall, imposing man with wide shoulders, every inch of him muscle. If he wanted to scare someone, he wouldn't have any trouble. Today he wore a forbidding expression, his body language aggressive.

"My name is Sheriff Ryan Parks. I'm the law in Plenty, Florida, and I wanted to make sure the press understands that we take our privacy and safety seriously in our town. We have an anti-stalking law that is heavily weighted toward the victim. If any of you or your fellow reporters come into town and try and take pictures of residents without their permission, you will be arrested and locked up. If you try and question or harass residents, you will be arrested and locked up. This also includes e-mail and texts. If you even look at somebody strangely, you will be answering to me. I will not have the safety and serenity of my town compromised by people who make their living off the misery of others. Do I make myself clear?"

He was scowling now and the room was dead silent. No one in their right mind would cross Ryan Parks in this mood.

He stepped down and joined her back in the hallway, giving her a smile. She grabbed his arm. "Since when do we have stalker laws that tough? I've lived in Plenty my entire life and never heard about those laws."

Ryan grinned. "Since this morning. Your men met with the town council and the laws were passed unanimously." He headed down the corridor. "Have fun and call Jillian when you get back to town."

Where the hell am I going?

She pressed her hand to her forehead, shaking her head. It was a lot to take in. Her men certainly were full of surprises today. Linc stood up, followed by Justin, and they walked out of the press room, turning her toward another long hallway. Linc leaned in and spoke softly to a man with a walkie-talkie.

"We're clear to go."

They didn't say a word as they led her to a back door where the SUV was waiting for them. She slid into the seat and they drove away, leaving downtown Orlando behind them, but not heading back to Plenty. She craned her neck to see the road signs.

"Okay, boys. You surprised me today, I'll give you that. It looks like the surprises aren't done. For the last and final time, will someone tell me where we're going?"

* * * *

Leah sounded frustrated and more than a little pissed off. It had been a huge gamble bringing her here, but they both decided they wanted her to see their relationship was the most important thing to them. It was more important than some golden-boy reputation he hated anyway.

Justin grabbed her hand. "We're taking you on a little vacation. We all need to get away for a few days."

Her eyes widened in shock. "What about the bookstore? What about clothes? I don't have any luggage."

Linc laughed but didn't turn from where he was driving. "Gabe and Alyssa are going to watch the store, so that's taken care of. Jillian and Ava went by your home and packed a bag for you. It's in the back of the truck with our luggage."

Leah pressed her lips together. She didn't look thrilled about their plans. Justin knew she was a little bit of a control freak, but he hoped she'd be so happy with their destination she'd let them off the hook.

Justin was starting to get worried. "Honey, are you mad at us? We just wanted to show you how much we love you. How important our relationship is to us. Did we do it wrong?"

Her expression softened. "No, you didn't do it wrong. It was tad dramatic, but it was the right thing to do. I'm just still in shock, I guess. I woke up this morning thinking it was going to be like every other day. It sure hasn't been."

Linc grimaced. "We tend to be dramatic at times, but we love you more than anything in the world. Are we okay?"

Leah smiled. "Yeah, we're okay. Just tell me one thing. How long have you been planning this? I never had a clue."

Justin grinned. "About a week. We've been talking to Zach and Chase Harper about the town passing a law keeping out reporters. They had actually suggested it when we first moved there, but we didn't think it was a big deal. It is now since we want to protect you and of course the entire town."

Linc nodded in agreement. "As for the press conference, it's been in the works since you gave the go-ahead to go public. We only needed to wait and see what Bobbi would do and get the town council business cleared away."

Bobbi had never gone through with her threat. It had been almost two weeks and they'd heard nothing else from her.

She shook her finger at Justin and Linc. "You're sneaky. I had no idea how sneaky you could be. All this was going on and I had no idea."

Justin laughed, leaning forward and capturing her finger with his teeth. "It's hard to be sneaky with a woman as smart as you. We have another surprise." He pointed to the airport signs they passed. "We're flying down to the Keys for a few days. We could use some rest and relaxation time. Just the three of us."

She ran her finger over Justin's lips. "I like the sound of that. Just the three of us."

* * * *

Her boys had wrapped a blindfold around her eyes and she was being led through the house they had rented for the weekend. It was a beautiful home in the Key West style with large windows to let in the light, and lush tropical landscaping around the patio and pool area. She was going to love spending a few days here with her men.

She walked cautiously, Justin holding her right elbow and Linc holding her left. The tantalizing smell of food teased her nostrils and mixed with the scents of the hibiscus. They'd led her outside of the house. They stopped and her blindfold was lifted from her eyes.

"Surprise!" Her men had huge grins on their faces, obviously pleased with themselves. A quick look around and she knew why. The pool area looked unbelievable. Candles were everywhere. On the table, at the base of plants, and floating in the pool. The table was covered with a white tablecloth and set for a romantic dinner, complete with champagne. There was a huge vase of tropical flowers as a centerpiece and she laughed as Linc snagged one, breaking off the stem, and tucking it behind her ear.

"You both were busy while I took a nap. A nap I didn't even really want, but was forced on me."

They'd insisted she lie down and she'd reluctantly taken them up on the offer. Obviously, they'd used the time well. She'd never seen anything more romantic.

"It's like something out of a romance novel," she breathed.

Justin and Linc beamed. Linc led her to the table and pulled out a chair for her.

"That's what we were going for. We figured we had a high bar to clear considering all the reading you do."

She looked around, still amazed at the effort they had gone to for her. "You cleared it. This is just beautiful. Thank you."

Justin popped open the champagne. "You're welcome. We're not the most romantic guys in the world, but we can make the effort for a special occasion."

Leah's heart sped up. "Is it a special occasion?"

Justin poured the golden liquid and handed her a fluted glass. "We hope so." He cleared this throat. "Leah, Linc, and I wanted you the moment we met you. You're everything we've ever dreamed of and hoped for. You're the only woman for us. We want a future with you."

Linc nodded. "We want forever with you. The question is—"

She hopped up, her champagne spilling all over her and them. "Yes! The answer is yes!"

Linc took the glass from her and set it on the table. "You don't even know what I was going to ask." He pulled her close to his warm body. "Maybe I was going to ask if you wanted to get a cat with us."

His lips were twitching and she wasn't fooled for a minute. "I'm not really a cat person. I'm more of a dog person. I'd get a dog with you."

Laughter spilled from Justin, his blue eyes shining. "She's not falling for it, buddy. She's onto us. How long have you known what we were going to ask, honey?"

It was her turn to laugh. "Since I helped you clean your office the other day and took a call from a jewelry store in Tampa that a ring you had ordered was ready to pick up. And technically, you haven't asked yet, by the way."

Linc slapped his forehead. "That's right. I asked you to help us straighten out the mess in the office." He kissed her hard on the lips. "We don't have to ask now. You already answered."

She pulled back and stuck out her lower lip, pouting. "I was just so excited." She ran her hands down their muscled chests, breathing in their arousing scents. She was so going to rip off their clothes very soon. "I love you both so much."

Justin rolled his eyes. "If we don't ask, we'll never hear the end of it." He fell to one knee and Linc followed. They both were smiling and looked gorgeous. She couldn't believe she was this lucky. She was going to get to spend her life with these men and be happy forever.

Linc pressed his lips to her knuckles. "Will you let us share the rest of your life, baby?"

"Will you let us love you forever, honey?" Justin asked.

She nodded, her throat tight with emotion. Linc slipped a ring on her left hand and she gasped when she saw it.

"It's blue."

They both stood, Justin picking up her hand and gazing at the ring. "It's a blue diamond. Quite rare. Just like you."

She blinked, tears welling in her eyes. "It's beautiful. I love it. I love you."

She kissed both of them in the flickering candlelight. "And they lived happily ever after."

She knew they would. Her men would write a story better than any she had ever read.

THE END

WWW.LARAVALENTINE.NET

ABOUT THE AUTHOR

I've been a dreamer my entire life. So, it was only natural to start writing down some of those stories that I have been dreaming about.

Being the hopeless romantic that I am, I fall in love with all of my characters. They are perfectly imperfect with the hopes, dreams, desires, and flaws that we all have. I want them to overcome obstacles and fear to get to their happily ever after. We all should. Everyone deserves their very own sexy, happily ever after.

I grew up in the cold but beautiful plains of Illinois. I now live in Central Florida with my handsome husband, who's a real, native Floridian, and my son whom I have dubbed "Louis the Sun King." They claim to be supportive of all the time I spend on my laptop, but they may simply be resigned to my need to write.

When I am not working at my conservative day job or writing furiously, I enjoy relaxing with my family or curling up with a good book.

For all titles by Lara Valentine, please visit
www.bookstrand.com/lara-valentine

Siren Publishing, Inc.
www.SirenPublishing.com

CPSIA information can be obtained at www.ICGtesting.com
Printed in the USA
LVOW04s1659140615

442438LV00022B/782/P